GW01167685

No part of this publication may be reproduced, stored in a retrieval system, or transmitted in any form or by any means, electronic, mechanical, photocopying, recording, scanning, or otherwise, without the prior written permission of the publisher, except in the case of brief quotations within critical reviews and otherwise as permitted by copyright law.

NOTE: This is a work of fiction. Names, characters, places, and incidents are a product of the author's imagination. Any resemblance to real life is purely coincidental. All characters in this story are 18 or older.

Copyright © 2019, Willow Winters Publishing. All rights reserved.

Seth
&
Laura

W Winters
USA TODAY BESTSELLING AUTHOR

"Monsters are real, and ghosts are real too. They live inside us, and sometimes, they win."

Stephen King

From USA Today bestselling author Willow Winters comes a heart-wrenching, edge-of-your-seat gripping, romantic suspense.

I ran from him, even though my heart knew better.
Love was one thing, but survival another.

He chose a life of crime. I never wanted any of it; I only wanted him. I left when the danger bled into my life, taking more than I was willing to sacrifice.

I should have known he'd come for me.
Men like him always get what they want.
The temptation in his eyes, the heat of his touch . . .
it's all still there, but his gaze is harsher now
and his grasp unrelenting.

He's not the boy I fell in love with, although pieces of what we once had are still there. I can feel it.
I know what he wants from me, and I know it comes with a steep price. I'll pay it though, if for no other reason than to touch him again. Just once more.

I'll close my eyes and forget about the risks that come with this life and with him. I only hope he doesn't do the same.

Desperate To Touch

Prologue

Laura

The first year Seth moved to the east coast years ago

The journal in my hand is thick and the edge of its pages are worn. As though she didn't just write in its pages daily, but instead read and reread the scribbled confessions of the past three years constantly. The spine itself is cracked and it divides the journal in two.

Guilt riddles its way into my thoughts. I shouldn't be reading a patient's journal, not when she only gave it to me because I told her I'd fix it for her. She trusted me because I'm her nurse. I'm supposed to help Delilah and take care of her.

The poor woman who lives on pills during the day and is haunted by nightmares when the sun sets gave me all her secrets.

I know I shouldn't take it, but the second half of the journal starts with the description of a barn Marcus took her to.

Marcus. Just seeing his name chills me down to my bones. I don't even realize that I've stopped moving, breathing, that I've simply halted in the middle of the narrow hall until a sweet new resident asks me if I'm okay. I think her name is Bethany.

"Fine," I tell her and force a smile, although the scribbled name, Marcus, lingers in my mind. The whispered hiss, Marcus, repeats itself faster and faster as I make my way to the office to read what she wrote about him. The Rockford Center deals with mental health, so naturally, drugs and violence are a conversation starter. Many of my patients talk about Marcus. Marcus and the Cross brothers. Recently, Seth King is a name that's going around too. I have to close my eyes, swallowing thickly as I shut the door to the dark office, leaning my back against it and simply trying to breathe.

Seth King, the man I loved on the other side of the country. The man I ran away from. He gave me time, but I knew he'd come for me. It's been a week since I first heard he was here, only miles from me, and I've been praying. I begged God to give me a sign, to tell me what to do. Opening my eyes, I stare down at the notebook. My salvation.

I photocopied every page of Delilah's journal, hiding in the small back office of the Rockford Center. I can still remember how anxious I was and how heat smothered every inch of my skin. Knowing I could be fired instantly, I still had to do it. I'd only just started working at the center, my first job as a nurse. I had to do whatever it took to survive. I suppose I'd been saying that a lot back then.

That journal was my leverage for when Seth inevitably came for me. Filled with multiple entries all about Marcus, the boogeyman, the Grim Reaper. A faceless villain who made deals in back alleys, running the streets around these parts, battling for power along with the Cross brothers. Unlike Carter Cross and his brothers, no one knows who Marcus is. They've never seen his face, but his signature power plays and ruthless reputation are notorious.

I thought that if Seth came for me demanding the money I stole, I'd give him the copies. I thought maybe it would be of value to him because I knew he came to work with the Irish mob who ruled this part of the East Coast, a.k.a. the Cross brothers. And they'd give anything to uncover any details on their faceless nemesis, Marcus, and his secrets.

They were all in the worn journal. This woman Delilah, my patient, had seen him. Felt him. She *loved* Marcus. She had a single journal when she was first admitted. It described details of where they met and what he wanted with her. It was leverage. Several years have passed; my patient's collection has grown as she's come in and out of the Rockford Center, when her mental state is too harmful to be away from the help we give her. She has a journal for every year, five years now, and I never stopped photocopying them. I could give Seth information on Marcus, in hopes that he wouldn't hold our past against me.

I kept waiting and waiting for Seth to come for me. Didn't he know he'd have to be the one to make the first move? I wouldn't even be able to look him in the eyes or say his name out loud.

Seth King.

Years came and went yet he never approached me. It wasn't relief I felt, it was like a prolonged mourning. Maybe he wanted me to feel his presence, to know I couldn't have him. I remember the first night that thought came to me, and how hard I sobbed against my pillow at the thought. I'd take my punishment; I deserved it.

Fate is a cruel sorceress, but this time I love her. Because last night, I saw him. I spoke to him. He called me *Babygirl* and even through the fear, I want him to say it again.

CHAPTER 1

SETH

She still doesn't know how badly she fucked me over.

I try to keep that in mind as I wait for Laura. Waiting for her is all I've done since she said good night two weeks ago. Each hour has felt like an eternity. She whispered it when she opened the back door of my car, sliding out with tears running down her cheeks. She never cried in the open; she hated the tears. "Useless" is what she used to mutter when she was on the verge of tears.

Back then I always held her while she let it all out. That night, fourteen days ago, I merely watched as she stayed as silent as she could, wiping the tears from her cheek. Maybe that's why she whispered "good night"—she didn't trust herself to speak too loud or else I'd realize she was crying.

I already knew though. She should know better than to think she can hide from me.

If she thinks I don't know how much it hurts, she's dead wrong.

The tick of the clock in Jase's office doesn't stop. It reminds me that I'm getting closer to seeing her again. She's to meet me, to come prepared to pay for the damages. She doesn't know though, just how much she fucked me over.

"Anything else on Walsh?" Jase questions his brother, Declan, as I sit in the corner chair, a dark leather wingback. I listen to the two of them go over the details Declan's been able to gather on the crooked cop hell-bent on revenge against the man known as Marcus. Only half my attention is on them. Until Declan says something about pitting the two of them against one another.

For a moment, I'm torn from my obsessive thoughts of seeing Laura tonight. The thoughts have been coming and going throughout the day. In the dark of night, alone in my bed with nothing but the memories of her, not a damn thing could get through to me. Certainly not sleep.

"Seth, what do you think?" Jase asks me, rolling up the sleeves of his crisp white dress shirt. Watching him lean back against his chair, the tailored suit jacket draped behind him, I'm reminded that I have shit to do other than deal with the woman who broke what semblance of a heart I had.

"I think being between the two of them is a piss-poor

place to be," I say, speaking up so Declan can hear me from where he is on the other side of the expansive office. His head is down as he types on the keys of his sleek laptop. It's state of the art and expensive as fuck with all the software loaded onto it. He's constantly searching for more information on Cody Walsh, the cop and former FBI agent who came to this town wreaking havoc.

"It would be easier if Walsh wasn't blackmailing us to help him find Marcus."

"It's not like we can give him Marcus anyway. He'll learn that it's not that easy," I comment but the foresight of what will happen along the way, and more importantly, after, breeds a disdain for the scheming cop. Months of surveillance on Marcus's men have given us nothing but a list of men who work for the man. Nothing about him in particular. We don't have a damn thing to give Walsh.

"Then how does him blackmailing us play out?" Jase's unspoken concerns are read easily with the worry in his expression. If we can't help Officer Walsh find Marcus, he could turn in the evidence he has on Jase and me. Then we're fucked.

"We need to get something on Walsh. We can't trust that he doesn't have backups of the tapes. We could bury ourselves helping him and in the end, he'd turn us in anyway."

"I agree with Declan," I say as I nod solemnly. My voice is even and calm. The threat of going away for murder is there...

but all I can focus on is Laura, and making her sweet ass pay for leaving me.

"Even if Walsh does turn in the evidence, we have ways to get around a conviction," Jase says and his menacing glare moves to the lit fireplace on the right side of the room. "As soon as we're able, I want him dead."

I used to feel chills at the thought of murder. They would climb up my spine, sending a freezing cold deeper into my blood as they crept their way up. Not anymore, though. It's been quite some time since I've felt any remorse or apprehension at the depravity I engage in.

"It must be done," I agree.

"When the time comes, we burn his house down, raid his office and get any evidence you can find."

"His car too," Declan adds. "He has PO Boxes in the upper east. Those need to be ransacked as well. All three of them."

"What the hell is he doing with those?" A crease settles deep between my brow.

"Maybe that's where he stores his evidence?" Jase questions, and a hopeful glint resurrects itself in his dark gaze. "Former FBI agents have their quirks and habits. We need to learn every single one of this prick's."

I only nod. There's no telling why Walsh does what he does. He seems to work alone, but the more we learn, the more is amiss. The evidence in his possession could put us away for murder. I'm not willing to allow that. Not when I just got Laura back.

No fucking way is some crooked cop getting in the way of my plans. I wish I had my crew here. For the first time in years, I feel like I truly need them. Maybe it's because Laura's back. Or maybe it's because the danger has a tighter grip around my throat. They're on the other side of the country, though. I haven't spoken to them in a long damn time.

I offer my suggestion and say, "We can put some men on the post office. See how often he goes to the PO Boxes, if ever."

"Agreed," Declan chimes in. "We need to watch him day and night. I can't find shit on him from the last three years and before that he was an agent so I don't trust it."

The ticking of the clock sounds with the crackling of wood and hiss of the fire as the three of us consider our reality. We're dealing with two pricks who have information on us, yet we're lacking when it comes to knowledge about them.

"All of our resources are going toward watching the army of a ghost," Jase says, referring to Marcus's men, "and to a fucking cop who could bring us down."

"We'll take care of it," I comment evenly and reassuringly, joining Jase to stare at the fire. Instead of seeing a cocked trigger, or the match that would cause an explosion, I see blue eyes in the flames. Parted lips. I swear I can hear Laura's moan.

"You all right, Seth?" The question doesn't come from Jase or from Declan. The office door creaks open as Carter steps in, his footsteps heavy as he enters.

"Fine," I answer Carter Cross, the oldest brother and rightful leader of this crew. His ruthlessness and reputation precede him.

He murmurs low and then takes in each of his brothers. "I think we should reconsider Marcus."

"Fuck Marcus." Jase's voice is harsh as he speaks. Marcus is the one who gave the cop the leverage. The bastard set us up. Walsh isn't the only one who wants to take Marcus down.

Carter merely smirks, the only hint of humor that's graced this office for months. He's taller than his brothers. Broader shoulders too with an air about him that's deadly. Jase could charm anyone; he's handsome and well spoken. Declan's quiet and smiles easily enough. Carter's harder, brutal. Even his jawline is harsh. Recently though, since he's found Aria, a different side of him is showing.

"Any unspoken truce we had with Marcus is gone," Jase continues, his anger getting the best of him. "He fucked with us on a personal level. He stole our supply, he captured—"

"All in the past. The enemy of our enemy is our friend."

"Which one, brother?" Jase's gaze narrows. His animosity for the two men shows without even the thinnest veil to hide behind. "You'd choose Marcus over Walsh? When Marcus is the one who set us up! He gave us over to Walsh when we did nothing to him. He's a traitor. I won't rethink a damn thing."

"Your emotions are getting the best of you." Carter's lack of emotion, his logical thinking combined with unforgiving lethal force, is what made the Cross brothers what they are. If nothing else, I admire it.

My gaze moves slowly between the two brothers, as does Declan's. I understand Jase's anger and his fear.

"What would you have us do?" Jase questions. Their dark gazes meet, and neither softens. Carter's hand falls in the pocket of his crisp black suit as he seems to debate an answer.

"Surveillance will take time. Do we have it?" he asks.

"Yes," Declan speaks up, cracking the tension but not breaking it. In gray slacks and a white Henley, Declan's attire makes him stand out from his brothers. He always does though. But it's his quiet, watchful nature that allows him to blend in with crowds. He doesn't have the same intensity about him that Jase and Carter do. At least not in public. I've seen him though. I've seen the real him and it's nothing like the man on the other side of the office.

Carter nods, running his thumb over his freshly shaven chin, the stubble already starting to show. He's a beast of a man, dressed up in a tailored suit.

"My only thought, and something I hope you would consider... if we get rid of Walsh, who will get rid of Marcus?" Carter questions and for a moment, Jase's head tilts as he considers his brother.

I'm nodding my head in short, nearly undetectable movements when Carter looks at me. I've found companionship with Jase, and friendship with Declan. Carter though has never allowed a step toward anything other than a working relationship. He's guarded, and until recently, I'd hardly spoken to him in the years I've worked for the Cross brothers. He'd be in the room, he'd speak. But not to me. Never to anyone other than his brothers. Guarded is a word that doesn't do him justice.

The trust simply isn't there. I respect that. I understand it more than he knows.

"You certain there's nothing you'd like to tell me?" Carter questions. "To tell *us*?"

A prickle of unease travels along my skin. Hot and sickening, but I answer calmly and with a no-nonsense tone. "Not a damn thing. If there's something you'd like to ask, I'll do as I've always done. I'll tell you whatever you want to know."

Declan and Jase are quiet as Carter squares his shoulders and contemplates a moment. "Something's going on with you," Carter finally speaks.

My palms are clammy as I clench and unclench my fists. "If you're doubting—"

"You are in this family. I don't doubt your loyalty or your ability... yet." Although Carter's tone is harsh, there's a softness I haven't seen from him before. *You are in this family*.

I am in no family. I haven't been for quite some time.

"Like I said, there's something going on with you." As Carter repeats the accusation, Jase leans back against his desk. The skin on his knuckles turns white as he grips the edge of it.

"Old ghosts," Carter surmises. "For weeks now."

Ever since I saw Laura with Bethany, Jase's girlfriend. I only nod, swallowing thickly.

"If something's going on—"

"It's personal," I reassure him and keep my tone even but without any room for discussion. "It won't get in the way of anything."

"If I've noticed the change, Seth… those ghosts are already in the way."

Chapter 2

Laura

I'm trying to remember everything Seth said two weeks ago, but all I can hear is *Babygirl*. All I can feel is the prick at the back of my eyes. *He asked me how I thought it would end...* that's right. That aching feeling in my chest returns and I swallow, dry and harsh as I sit in my car. My seatbelt's off and the constant pinging from the dash is driving me crazy until I pull the keys out of the ignition.

I begged for his forgiveness while all he did was stare at me through the rearview mirror. I tried to explain, but his gaze remained brutal and unforgiving. I put my hand on his shoulder once, and that was the only time he really looked at me. First my hand, and then into my eyes.

He wrote down an address, this address. In the note, he

told me to come in two weeks—which has felt like forever. And he gave me a time... five minutes from now.

Don't make me come for you.

I read the line noting how quickly my heart beats, then the pause and the sudden shortness of breath. A wave of overwhelming emotions crashed down around me. The thought of him coming for me will always make me feel conflicted. I want to run from him, but I also want him to capture me, to force me to stay. Because I'm selfish, just like my heart is when it ticks and skips like it's running and it's out of breath.

I stopped taking my medication for arrhythmia when I got settled here. My hand instinctively hovers over my chest as the *thump*, *thump*, *thump* goes off beat. With my eyes closed, I breathe in deep and tell it to calm down.

I haven't needed a pill in years. Seth King fucks up my heart. No one can tell me otherwise. It's all his fault.

Ping.

Jolting from the buzz on my lap, as I sit in the car outside of the address Seth gave me, I silently scold myself. *Calm the fuck down.*

The heat from the vents hits my face and I'm quick to flick the button off. It's cold for an autumn night, colder than it's been since March if I remember right, and the wind is unforgiving too.

With the blush of the sunset on the horizon, I'm close to a

moment I knew would come one day. For better or for worse. I'm safe in my car... safe for now.

It took me twenty-five minutes to drive here. All in silence. That's all it took. It felt like forever, but forever is over far too quickly now that I'm sitting here staring at the massive house. It's all old light gray stone with dark blue roofing... the slabs all the way up there look like stone too. It's hard to tell this late at night though. There are two stories with a wraparound porch. There isn't a piece of furniture at all outside though. The old Victorian has been cared for. It's obviously been meticulously maintained, which must take effort given that it's out here, surrounded by miles and miles of woods.

Taking my gaze away from the gorgeous house, I read the text and then I have to read it again.

You want to go out soon?

My brow furrows, a deep line settling in my forehead.

My first thought is: *what is Cami doing on the East Coast?* After all, who else would be texting me?

A vise tightens around my dry throat. *Cami's dead.* Fuck, my head is so messed up.

It's been like this since I saw Seth days ago. Since he called me Babygirl. The past has a way of creeping in. All the things once forgotten come back. With the pain lingering in my chest, oh how I wish Cami were here. I wish it were her who sent that text.

It's been a long time since I've had moments like I've been

having, where I've forgotten about everything that happened when I left. I don't hold the guilt or any of the fear. In those moments, my mind plays tricks on me to convince me Cami's still alive, still happy. I've only left her on the other side of the country for school and work. It's a nice thought for a moment, but then my eyes prick with hot tears and the memory of the night I left comes flooding back in a rush.

I'll never forget that imagery. I'll never forget how cold her skin was. Or the feel of her lashes against my fingers when I closed her eyes. I hold my fingers now, willing the sensations to go away.

My body's heavy as I fall against the driver seat. Breathe in, breathe out. Just keep breathing.

Ping. Bethany texts again. She's not Cami. She'll never be Cami.

A new friend to replace me, Cami's voice whispers in my head and my throat tightens as I read the text Bethany sent: *I miss you. I really do.*

I don't even have time to think about what happened between Bethany and me. I haven't seen her since she left my apartment, pissed off at me. I did what I had to do. It was a few days after I'd seen Seth. I did what I thought was right.

I'll tell her everything. She'll understand. Some friendships come and go but some, like the one I have with Bethany, are meant to be forever friendships. I want so badly to make it up to Bethany and explain. Just like I want to do with Seth.

She'll understand.

Failure and regret are kneading together in the pit of my stomach. I've made so many mistakes. Countless times I've prayed and wished that I could just go back so I could do things differently. If only I could have known...

I miss you too and whenever you want, I'm there. I type out my response and hope she can feel just how much I miss her too.

Tonight? Bethany's answer is immediate and my teeth bite into my bottom lip as I suck in a deep breath.

Dammit. I can't tonight.

Tomorrow then? she asks.

Tomorrow. I respond immediately and then quickly add, *I am all yours tomorrow.*

I don't realize I'm holding my breath until she replies, *Can't wait* and I finally exhale.

I can make things better. I can make them right again. Closing my eyes again, I see Cami's face. *Not everything can be made right.*

With another exhale, I try to shake off the nerves that curl and coil around my insides. Preparing to toss my keys in my bag, the jingle of them is all I can hear other than my wonky heart when I look up and see Seth standing there.

My heart tumbles over itself at the sight of him. I've only seen him in a suit once before. For his father's funeral. Back then, the suit looked like a hand-me-down. He could have afforded whatever suit he wanted, but he chose a loose black one, with a black tie that was never tight around his throat. The knot hung loose and the second the casket was lowered to the ground, he ripped it off, followed by his jacket. It was snowing that day, but he couldn't have cared less. He never did like suits.

It seems that time has changed all that. The expensive cloth is cut perfectly to fit Seth's broad shoulders. The black is pristine, the cufflinks a detail I'd never envisioned on him. He lifts his arm just slightly, glancing down at his wrist and the shine of a silver watch, or maybe platinum, reflects back at me.

His clothes are all wrong, all different from what I know about the boy I fell in love with. But his eyes, they're the same. His stubble and hard jaw, they're what I remember. His cheekbones seem more defined with how trim he keeps his facial hair and the lines around his eyes are faint, but they tell tales of an older man, not one in his twenties. The look he's giving me though, with his lips slightly parted, his tongue peeking out just for a moment to wet his bottom lip... it's reminiscent of before, but just like his clothes, it's worn differently.

Skip, trip, thump. He doesn't stop staring as I take him in. Like he's waiting for something. My heart responds but I don't. I'm as still as can be in my seat, feeling the heat the car has stopped providing even without it being on anymore. It engulfs me as Seth's stare penetrates through everything.

He doesn't stand there for long, his large hands clenched into fists at his sides. They unclench and his right smooths down the black pressed suit pants he's wearing. Irritation grows in his expression, but I'm in no rush to move.

I hate how he looks at me, but I love that he's looking at me at all.

I reach out to the passenger seat without breaking Seth's gaze before he can open the door himself. He's hiding from me. Behind those blue eyes, I see nothing anymore. Maybe a hint of lust and a wall of hate, but not him. I don't see him anymore and it fucking hurts. It's a jagged rip to my heart.

Before I step out, I reach behind me for my purse; inside it is the notebook. Only the first one though. I didn't bring them all.

As I stand toe to toe with him, swinging the thin black strap of my blush satchel over my shoulder and feeling the gust of wind send a chill down my spine, I close the car door without looking back. The thudding click of it shutting is all I can hear. Even the woods that surround us are silent.

It's hard to believe Seth's right in front of me. The wave of heat from his hard body towering over me is addictive. He's so close that his scent fills my lungs and it brings memory after memory as I stand breathless in front of him. I could touch him; I know I could.

He could touch me if he wanted to as well. Neither of us moves though.

"I told you not to make me come for you." His deep voice is a low baritone, a threat not so veiled laying within the syllables.

What was left of the light from the sun is waning and the moon doesn't provide a damn thing tonight. The shadows come quicker than they have any other night. My God, does the darkness make Seth look even more tempting. Fear is ever present, the unknowing and lack of control driving my anxiety to pump my unbalanced heart harder.

I pay it all no mind. Seth is here in front of me.

"Did you hear me?" he asks, although it's not a question. It's more a statement of his discontent.

"I'm sure that's not what you meant in that note, Seth," I finally speak, my voice more even than I dreamed it would be. How it comes out so calm and collected, I have no idea.

Goosebumps line my arms as another gust of wind pushes at my back, gathering my hair and causing it to tumble over my shoulders. I cross my arms as my nipples pebble.

"I'm here," I tell him. As if stating the obvious was needed.

The anger and edge of threat are absent, and the heat in Seth's eyes roars when he glances down my body and then back to my own wandering gaze.

Time passes, too much of it, before I break the silence and break our caught stares to say, "I didn't make you come far, did I?"

Chapter 3

Seth

She's here. Laura's in my grasp. And she's completely unaffected. I can't fucking take it. It's a black hole that whirls around me. Nothingness, yet I'm falling. Hard and fast.

This gut-wrenching concoction of desire and anger, betrayal and longing... it's too much. I can't focus on any one aspect of this moment. Control feels like a concept I can't grasp as the blood rushing in my ears drowns out everything else.

Closing my eyes, I inhale long and deep. She is the woman I used to love. When I was someone else. Nothing more. I try to convince myself of that truth.

Her words linger, confirming the statement.

I didn't make you come far, did I?

Her comment pisses me off more and more with every

step I take toward the house. The anger laces with desire. Her smart mouth has always gotten me hard.

I gently place my splayed hand on her back, to lead her into my house, hiding my eagerness.

Inside. I need to get her inside.

I can barely feel her, but I don't miss how her eyes close at my touch. All it takes is a gentle push and Laura walks fast enough so that I barely have contact with her.

The soft satin of her red dress caresses my fingertips. I know she's cold in the thin material. She chose this dress, tight around her ass and low cut, for a reason. Everything she does is for a reason.

Every step closer to the door, I gather more and more composure. I remember who I am today and not what we had before.

The past needs to stay where it is. Those ghosts are long gone. Carter's assessment follows me, hardens me... it warns me to be careful.

As Laura passes the threshold, I notice her long hair, once naturally dark but now lightened, falling over one shoulder. She peeks over her shoulder but not at me though; instead she looks back to her car. Maybe second-guessing everything, maybe wanting to run. I wonder if she can feel the difference inside of me. I feel it every damn day. I'm highly aware that I'm not the same man she remembers from the past. How could I be? That night changed everything about me.

When she chose to run, so did something inside of me. And it never came back.

The clack of the front door closing is followed by the lock clicking into place. Laura's body shudders at the sound, and I watch closely as her plump lips, colored the same dark red as her dress, part as she sucks in a breath. She may not want to admit I've gotten to her, but I damn well know I have.

She can pretend to be the confident seductress when she looks in the mirror. But I see underneath it all.

The mix of dark woods and grays, all the masculine clean lines of my home is at complete odds with Laura. She stands out, unable to hide in the neutrals of the open floor plan. She aims to move to the sleek ashen davenport sofa in the living room. Even picking up her pace, turning the air between us businesslike, she takes a few steps forward, only for me to catch her elbow and move her forward, toward the office.

Her quick glance and questioning gaze are gone as quickly as they came. I couldn't give two shits where we do this, but she won't decide it.

She decided to run from me. To steal from me. She doesn't get to decide anything else.

Never fucking again. She doesn't have a choice.

I've had countless days to plan what I'd say and do. Years ago, back in California. And years here, knowing she was close enough to see with only minutes of driving. Even as I walk her through the hall and open the carved walnut office door, ushering her inside, the plan is changing.

Some days it's a debt owed and I want her to pay me back, however I choose.

Some moments the hate for her leaving me at my worst is so strong, that I don't want a damn thing to do with her. I want her to know how close I am, and to know I don't care enough to seek her out.

Smelling her sweet scent, and listening to the steady beat of her heels clicking against the wood, part of me wants to charm her, to beg for her forgiveness and offer her the world. I could give her that. Everything is different now. That part comes with something else. It starts as an inkling of sorrow, but it's quick to spread, like oil slicking across the water. It's thin, but covers every inch in blackness. I want to beg her to love me again. I want her to see how wrecked I was. How I feel like nothing without her. I am nothing anymore, but why would she want me? Why the hell would she ever come back?

She makes me weak.

"Your home is lovely," Laura comments politely with her slender back to me as I shut the office door. Both of her hands grip the strap of her purse, giving away the nerves she's hiding. "The inside isn't like the outside... it's so modern and open."

I'm different; I know I am, but so is she. We're nothing like we used to be. I assess her as she appraises my office. Taking in the rows of books, organized by date of publication. I collect the rare ones because I like the way they smell and look, but I haven't read them. I don't intend to either.

Her footsteps are gentler in this room and the angular edges of her dress seem to soften as I watch her move from one end of my small office to the other. Her footsteps are muted although it's hardwood beneath her heels. She's walking more carefully, with more hesitation.

I love that. The façade fades as the seconds pass.

She's still the same girl I know, even if she wants to appear otherwise.

Her hair is curled, meticulously so when she still sat in her car. But the wind has seen to ruffle her blond tresses. I like her even more with her hair slightly messy. She should aim for that next time, a "just recently fucked" look.

I want to ask her why she did it, why she dyed her hair. It's gorgeous on her; she has the tan in her skin to pull it off. I love the memory of her from before more though. She was perfect before.

Her nails are painted a darker shade of red than the short dress that hugs her curves. Even her makeup is flawless. It's obvious this look—this sex kitten appeal, is deliberate.

I would like to pretend she did it for me. But two weeks ago, she looked similar. Perfectly put together and dressed with an edge of a vixen. The thought hits me as she glances up at me: *this is who she is now*.

Is it a lie? Is she still the woman I fell for?

Laura turns the moment my eyes read hers, preventing

me from imagining running the tip of my finger along her skin. From the crook of her neck, all the way down her back. I could see myself doing it again and again until she begged me to unzip her dress. "Did you decorate it yourself?" Again, she's polite.

I fucking hate niceties.

"I hired someone," I say and my answer comes out flat as my eyes gauge her expression. Her knuckles are white from her tight grip, but her smile is forced. The longer the seconds draw out, the tighter her grip gets.

Maybe she's realizing what I am. Maybe she's come to the conclusion that she doesn't trust the man I've become. I wouldn't blame her.

I take my time, slipping off my jacket and folding it neatly before placing it over the arm of an amber leather executive chair in the corner of my office. The cufflinks are next to go, sitting them on the end of the antique bookshelf to the left of my desk. I focus on them, avoiding Laura's prying eyes although I can feel them on me. Every step I take circles her as I move closer to where she is until I finally look up at her, feet away, but I feel miles apart with the way she looks at me.

"Are you scared of me?" I ask her and take a step forward. She doesn't move from where she is in front of my desk. "Maybe of what I may tell you?" I take another step forward, blocking the light from the floor lamp in the far corner and causing shadows to darken her face. "Or maybe what I may do to you?"

"If you wanted to hurt me, you would have already," she answers me with such certainty, although it's practically whispered.

She doesn't say anything else; she doesn't give a hint of what's she's thinking or feeling. She doesn't apologize. She doesn't ask me for anything. The tension thickens as she waits for a response from me.

How long would she have lived without me and been perfectly fucking fine? All the while, I've died inside.

"You stole from a criminal," I practically hiss. "So many others would have killed you simply to set an example."

"You didn't tell them," she responds without letting a second pass. I had so much left to say, so much to make her feel the anxiousness I feel. It vanishes when her gaze softens with agony. "You didn't tell them I took the money. Your crew never knew." The sound of her swallowing mixes with the desperation in her voice. My gaze falls to her slender neck and then drifts down to the dip below her throat. She must have difficulty breathing now, because her lips part just to inhale and she leaves them that way. Her chest rises and falls and finally she takes a half step back.

"Derrick?" I ask her and she nods slowly, bringing my attention back to her face. Her expression gives nothing away, even if her posture gives away everything. "What else?"

"What else what?" she questions, again evenly.

"Tell me everything Derrick told you."

"We haven't spoken in a long time," she says then breaks my gaze as the corners of her lips pull downward. Looking behind her, she rests against the edge of the desk, setting her purse beside her. Her hands tremble slightly until she clasps them together, hiding her emotions as she pretends to relax in front of me.

What a lie she's become. Or is it only for me? Sucking in a breath, I rip my gaze away from her and wait for her response. "Tell me."

"The last time I talked to him was a few years ago, when you first moved here."

"So you've known—" I start to say, and it comes out like an accusation.

"That you've been here?" she says as she cuts me off and I only nod. "I knew when you started working with the Cross brothers because of the whispers. I called Derrick and he confirmed it."

"What did he say?" I shouldn't feel this heat in my blood. This apprehension that she may not like what Derrick told her. I'm not here to soothe her or comfort her though. That's not what this is about.

I will never let her in like I did before. Never again. I learned my lesson. She made sure of that.

"He only said you heard about the Cross brothers and how quickly they were taking over... I asked him if you came for me." Her voice hitches for the first time and she has to swallow thickly before continuing. I watch pain flash across her expression and she doesn't try to conceal it. "He said you didn't."

Tap, tap. My pointer finger rests on the desk as I lean my thigh against the side of it opposite from her. *Tap, tap.* I wonder if that hurt her. *Tap, tap.* I watch her face as she waits for me to say something, but I don't.

"I came up with a plan when I heard you were here," she confesses.

"A plan?"

"I had information I thought you'd want." I don't respond to her comment. I merely stare in her doe eyes, watching the way the gentle gold flecks among the blue brighten with emotions in their depths.

"Like a deal? You wanted to make a deal with me?" Anger roils inside of me, overwhelming my focus. *A deal to get me to leave her alone.*

"Yes," she whispers this time and her fear isn't something she can hide, judging by how she inches away from me.

"You thought I came to hurt you?" I question her.

"At first."

I ignore my immediate reaction to hearing her admit that. "I have a deal too. I've thought of a lot of them over the past few years."

"What's your deal?" she asks and lifts her chin slightly, her bright blue eyes boring into mine. Back to business maybe. I'm not sure what's going on in that pretty little head of hers.

"You do everything I say."

Her eyes search mine until she blinks rapidly and looks past me, shaking her head. "That's not a deal."

My words echoing in my head sound more and more inviting. "Yes, it is."

"What do I get in return?" She licks her lips quickly, leaning forward as if she's scrambling to hold on to something before adding, "Deals have two parties."

"You get to live," I offer her in all seriousness. I don't care who she's become. Laura's mine. I will get everything I want from her. I *need* it.

"I'm already living."

"You stole from me. There's a debt owed and a corresponding punishment. I would never let someone else steal from me and live."

"Just kill me then," she says and her voice cracks although she's quick to clear her throat. "Just kill me if that's what you want." Despite her shattered veneer she holds her head high. She accepts my glare and doesn't falter, her eyes brimming with tears.

Before I can respond, she says something else. I don't hear it though as I take a seat; I simply watch as she pulls herself back together. She's damn good at it. *At not needing me.*

I take my time, giving her a moment to breathe. At the head of the desk, I grip the armrests, waiting.

"Did you hear what I said?" Her composure is back,

although her breathing is ragged.

"You said you wanted an exchange. You want to change the details of our deal."

Her doe eyes beg me to consider, and they hold a vulnerability that her tense curves fail to deliver. As she takes a step forward, I think she wants to sit in the other wingback chair, but her legs give out. She grips both arms of the chair across from me as her chest rises and falls with a quickened pace. She can't hide the fear of coming back to this life. *Of coming back to me.*

As her bottom lip slips between her teeth, I note that she can't hide the desire either.

"I've wanted this for too long to consider your proposal," I tell her, spreading my legs wider and leaning forward in the wingback chair opposite hers. My elbows rest on my knees as I lean closer to her, only inches away as I whisper, "You know what I want. I want you."

"I can give you something you want more," she speaks clearly, although her last words waver when her gaze drifts to my lips.

Lies. There's nothing I want more.

I would have told her that and meant it with every bone in my body, but then she tells me, "I can give you Marcus."

LAURA

What would he do to me?

Even as I reach in my satchel for the notebook, my hand trembles. I can't imagine Seth hurting me. I can't. Even as he looks at me the way he does. That's not what scares me.

I'm scared to go back, back to him and all this shit he comes with. I don't want this life. I've never wanted it.

A voice in the back of my head whispers: *you're afraid to fall in love with him again.* I ache for him. So deeply. Agony shreds me when I see who he's become. I want to cry more than anything. I don't know how I'll survive this. All I have to cling to is a collection of photocopied pages, as if they'll save me from this.

"You're lying," he says and his voice is firm.

"I'm not; I haven't lied. I can give you information on Marcus."

"Yes you have," he bites out quickly and for the first time since I've been in here, I see a flash of sadness in his dark cobalt gaze. I can't respond to him. Not even when he turns away from me, leaning back and tapping his index finger on the desk again. He's so broken. I didn't do this to him. It's not because of me. With the notebook of photocopied pages between my fingers, I lie to myself again: *I didn't do this to him.*

"There's a patient at the Rockford Center. She's been in and out of there for years although she's not a resident currently,"

I explain as I hand over the notebook. It's a hardcover, black and nondescript, of her first collection of memories. Holding out the bound pages, I can't look in Seth's gaze. I can't and I won't, but he doesn't take it. He doesn't accept it and with every long second that passes, it only hurts more. "She's been with Marcus. She knows about him."

"Many people work for—"

"*Been* with," I interrupt him to emphasize, "she was his lover."

His fingers graze mine as he takes it. A hot and longing need for him is threatening to consume me. With my eyes closed, I try to ignore what the rough feel of his touch does to me. It's like a sparkler, hot and brightly lit, yet quickly extinguished. A part of me yearns to move forward, to light my entire body. I've always been weak for him. My soul in love with his, needing his. I keep my eyes closed even when I hear him turn the pages.

I left this man years ago but in this moment, it feels like I'm leaving him again. Simply because I refuse to give in. It feels like I'm running although I'm merely standing still in front of him.

"She wrote detailed descriptions of every location he took her."

"We have intel on his habits and the locations of his businesses." Seth speaks calmly, as if the information gathered in front of him is nothing new. With my eyes widening, I finally look at him, and then my body jumps when he tosses the heavy notebook down on his desk. The slap ricochets through my body.

"Like I said," he says and my gaze falls to his throat, watching the cords tense as he swallows and adds, "you'll do everything I say."

"There are more," I tell him quickly, ignoring his statement and even I can hear how begging my tone is.

I've fallen for this man once. If I do it again, I'll cross the point of no return. I'm sure of it.

His gaze is hungry as he exhales with disdain. "Give me all of them," he commands.

"I don't have them with me."

"You'll bring them next time then," he says. He's bossing me around and telling me what to do.

"I'll do what I please," I bite out, remembering who I am.

Seth smirks at my response, appearing not at all flustered.

"It will please you," he tells me and his tone is different. His cadence caresses every inch of my skin. Leaning forward, he rests his hand on my knee, and damn does my body respond to him. "I will make sure of that."

"Seth," I breathe his name.

"There are other things that need to be done first. I plan on taking my time."

Seth

Hearing her whisper my name like that...

I want her more than I will ever admit. Just like I'll never admit how dire the situation is with Marcus. I don't have this information, but she'll give it to me.

I burn for her to give me many things before that happens.

Her pain as I punish her. And her pleas for me to take her back.

One thing I'd planned to do since I moved back, one thing that has never deviated is sitting right behind her in the top drawer on the other side of the desk.

She watches me all the while and I wonder what she sees. What she thinks. What she feels. The drawer slides out with a creak and it's the only sound in the office.

For a split second, I wonder if I should do it. If I should give it back to her. Laura needs to feel it though. She needs to know.

With the folded paper in my hand, I take a moment to clear off the left side of my desk, slipping a pile of folders inside the drawer. Now all that's left is my laptop and a few odds and ends. The steel pen container is moved first. I set it on the windowsill behind me; clearing off what remains on the desk will take less than a minute. I want her ass right here, on this desk, once she's done reading what I'm holding.

"This is for you." I hand her the note, not going back on

the promise I made to myself, although I know without a question of a doubt, that she'd get up on this desk right now with no hesitation. She needs that note first. I told myself for years that if ever I were to see her again, she needed to have it back. There's dried blood on the edge of one side although it's turned a dark brown now. There are other stains on the once clean paper as well. I can still see right where she'd cried and the paper took in her tears, seeping into the crisp creased folds and warping them. It's harder to see it now though. It blends in with all the other evidence that the paper has existed for far too many years.

I watch her eyes as she unfolds the note. I watch her pupils dilate and note their glossy sheen as she rips her gaze away and looks anywhere but at me.

Her inhale is ragged and sharp.

"This isn't for me."

"It is. It's for you to read. I've read it enough."

The paper crinkles in her hand. The creases are so soft; I didn't think it could crinkle anymore.

She needs to be reminded that she told me she'd love me forever.

She promised me she would. She can read it and know it every day of her life like I have since she left me.

"I want you to read it every day. It's only fair—it's what I did for years."

Her voice is raw when she answers the command with,

"At least you had a note," and then tosses it onto the desk. Like she doesn't want it.

I didn't want it either. It would have been so much easier without it. If she'd just left me because she hated me.

"Is this what you want?" she asks as a tear rolls down her cheek, unable to hide it any longer. She angrily wipes it away.

"Partly," I admit out loud and shock myself. Her disgust shows and she grabs her purse this time, as if she'll leave.

"Sit down," I command as her ass lifts from the seat. She stills where she is. Debating maybe. "We aren't finished, Babygirl." I meant for the word to get to her. Not to me. But it settles in my chest, spreading the ache I've been doing my damnedest to suppress.

She's slow to take her seat, but she does.

"Want to know what I missed?" I ask her although at this point, I'm just speaking my mind. No filter; I let it all out. "The way you say my name," I say and close my eyes, focusing for a moment on the motions of my thumb. *Tap, tap.* "I missed it."

Even with my eyes closed, I can feel hers on me. I swear my body knows hers. The vulnerability of it all wanes as I flick through the scenes of what happened when she left.

"I missed the taste of you," I comment lowly and tilt my head when I look back at her. Her skin is a gorgeous blush color and her pale blue eyes are rimmed with a pink that matches her complexion. Desire dances between us. My cock hardens and her thighs tense as her inhale skips.

"I remember thinking one night," I say and point to the desk, "as I read that note, is any pussy that good?" Hardening my voice, I remind her of the anger.

She needs to be punished. She has to be.

Her red-rimmed eyes fill with lust. There's an undeniable heat.

"I want to taste you, Laura," I say and then realize it's not a command. She needs to be told what to do though. And every action reinforced.

Desire outweighs the rage. It outweighs everything. The image of her under me, her thighs parted, enters my mind. It's all I can focus on. With my zipper pressing tight against my erection, I get up from the chair and tell her to strip. I add, "I want you down to nothing."

I think, for a moment, there's no way she'll do it.

"Say please," she retaliates, although it's softly spoken and submissive, laced with a sadness too. A new roar of fire ignites inside of me.

"Please," I say and my voice comes out deeper, from a raw place inside of me as I lean forward, "Get your ass up here."

The hesitation in her expression is clear, but that doesn't stop her from toeing off her heels. She's quick to obey me. The hope that blooms from that knowledge is unwanted.

"I want you here," I say and splay my hand on the space to my left I cleared moments ago. All but the notebook and my laptop, which I move now, keeping my head turned as I go and pretending like I'm not obsessed with the peripheral image of her doing exactly what I tell her to do.

The balls of her feet pad on the floor as she makes her way around to the other side of the desk, climbing on top of it. Her heavy breathing invades my senses and fuels the rapid pump of my heart. She's naked, and I'm fully dressed. I swear if I were to move even a muscle right now, I'd take her, savagely and roughly on top of my desk.

Control. I grasp for it. I cling to it when her gaze searches mine for direction. I won't be reckless with her. That's why I lost her. Recklessness.

"Put your ass here and spread your legs." My voice is even and she listens, bringing the sweet scent of her femininity closer to me. I don't move, watching her crawl closer to position herself with her legs in front of her and her ass only inches from my hand on the desk.

My head falls to the side as she places one heel to the left of my hand. I let my nose brush against her calf, then kiss the inside of her knee.

"Seth." She calls my name as if she's falling and I don't respond. Not for a moment and then another. I'm waiting for that other heel to be placed and her thighs to part for me.

It takes her a long minute to do it, but she does.

She's propped up with her hands bracing her. Her breasts are small but they fall heavy, swaying slightly as she breathes.

Bringing my hand to her heat, I brush my knuckles against her soft flesh and then higher up her body, until my hand is at her stomach. "Down," I command, pressing against the base of her sternum and pushing her to lie on her back.

Her body burns under my touch.

"You shaved," I comment as I move my fingers back down. With both hands, I spread her thighs farther apart and she doesn't protest in the least.

"You shaved, you chose a dress and heels, but you came ready to bargain." I'm barely conscious of my own words as I stare at her pussy. Her clit is swollen and she's already glistening with desire. I run my middle finger between her lips, playing with her, toying with her cunt and watching goosebumps spread along her skin.

"You had to know I'd take you, didn't you?" I ask her. The way I'm seated, I can't see her eyes. I'm glad for that because it means she can't see my expression when she gasps as I push my finger inside of her.

She whispers the words, "I missed you too."

A painful recognition spreads through me, suffocating me, knowing it's true; it hurts to hear her say that even more. I lean down and take a languid lick, ignoring the longing in her response and focusing on how her back arches.

She's hot and sweet. I lap at her, taking my time, from her entrance to her clit. A strangled moan fills the air along with the sound of her nails scratching on the desk. As if she wants to grab hold of something.

Letting a low groan come from my chest, I enjoy her, drawing this out. Her thighs close in on me when she writhes on the desk and it's only then that I pull back.

She won't get off. I won't let her. I want her to miss it. To miss how I would do this to her the way I missed it.

"You don't get to cum. Not until I decide you should."

Standing up quickly, I push the chair back just as it nearly falls. I turn my back to her and when I hear her draw in a sharp breath, I tell her to stay.

"Don't you dare move." My heart pounds against my rib cage; maybe it's desperate to get back to her. A cold sweat lines my skin. "You do what I say and when," I state, reminding her of our arrangement.

"I told you no to that deal," she whispers, the desire still coloring her upper chest, throat and cheeks. She doesn't move though. I watch her to make sure she listens. Her eyes are closed as I slowly pace, ignoring her comment about her telling me no. I grab her throat with my right hand, feeling the pulse of her hot blood as she quickly looks up at me, wide eyed and full of concern.

"I missed that mouth of yours," I comment and then lean down, kissing her harshly. I expect it to be short lived, but when she parts her lips ever so slightly, even with the taste of her still present on my tongue, I deepen it. And she does the same.

There has always been a disconnect with us. Our bodies do one thing; our minds tell us another. With the fever of lust covering every inch of my skin, I pull away from her, although my grip on her throat is unmoving.

"You'll stay with me," I say absently, telling her without thinking and my mind plays tricks on me. It goes back years ago. If only she'd stay with me.

"No," she answers weakly, a raw vulnerability lacing the single word.

"You will and you'll pay off the debt with your cunt." I grasp for any reason at all for her to agree. To remember her guilt.

"Don't be crass," she bites out even as her voice trembles. She seems to come out of it, out of the haze of longing. Wiping the corners of her mouth, she stares back at me, not giving in to my demand. "I won't do it, Seth."

"Crass? Are you too good for that kind of language now?"

Even at my mercy, Laura's strength shines through. I wonder what she looked like when she left me. I wonder if she cried. Derrick swore to me there's no way she left without falling apart. I want to see her fall apart. I want to know what this version of her looks like when she does.

"I'm not yours anymore," Laura tells me calmly, still lying spread on my desk. The taste of her is still present on my tongue.

"You owe me," is all I tell her, firm and deliberate.

"You owe me too," she whispers after a moment and the crack in her guard splinters. Suddenly, she looks all too familiar. I have to let her go. In an instant, the room feels colder. The ghost of her in my living room stares back at me. Cross-legged on the floor with the scent of smoke filtering through my lungs.

"I owe you?" I question with feigned disgust. She's quick to sit up, to cover herself from me. The moment is lost. "What is it I owe you?" I dare her to answer me. To bring up her home, to bring up Cami. Fuck.

If she'd listened to me, if only she'd stayed close—I could have kept her safe. It could have been different. It didn't have to end the way it did.

I'm so close to screaming the words. *It didn't have to end like it did. You should have listened to me.* So close, I can feel them scratching up the back of my throat.

"I wish I'd never fallen in love with you," she admits and scrambles to get off my desk. *Stay still*, I warn myself. *Stay still.* If I move, I'll grab her. She reaches for her clothes, heedlessly throwing them on.

"You will stay with me. You will do everything I tell you to." I give the commands as if all of her objecting will vanish. I still don't trust myself to move. I swear I'll lift her beautiful ass over my shoulder and lock her in a room.

"You wanted to humiliate me? To prove to me you could still have me if you wanted?" she questions with disdain and the thought of what she's implying had not once occurred to me. Not once. I didn't even know until a moment ago that I could have her.

"You have no idea what I want from you!" I don't know why I scream. I don't know why I shake as she zips up her dress and slowly faces me.

"Yes, I do, and I'll tell you right now, Seth, it won't happen. I won't let it."

"I left you alone for years. I won't any longer," I tell her and my words are rushed.

"I'm not a plaything. I'm not yours anymore," she tells me as she grabs her heels from the floor.

"Yes. You are. That is exactly what you are."

She turns from my heated gaze, frantically looking for her purse until she can snatch it, ready to leave me.

"You'll come back tomorrow night. Five o'clock," I say calmly even as a panic stirs in my blood watching her race out of the door.

I don't follow her. I stay perfectly still, not trusting myself to move. It's not until I hear her car start from outside that I brace myself against my desk. It's still warm from where she laid herself bare for me.

The rev of her engine and the peeling out of her tires comes and goes until I'm alone.

She left me again. My eyes catch sight of the note on my desk. She left me again.

With a roar ripped from my throat, I grab the floor lamp and slam it against the bookshelf. Heaving in the darkened room, I can't let go of it.

She left me again, but she'll be back.

I'll have her again.

She'll be back.

Chapter 4

Laura

The bags under my eyes still feel heavy. I put on enough concealer to hide them though. I'm an expert at that now. I doubt anyone in this coffee shop can tell how much I cried last night.

With the small chatter and the subtle pop music, no one in Baked and Brewed is paying me any mind. I picked a table in the back corner and from here I can see everything in this place. It's cute and quaint, smelling of freshly brewed coffee and cinnamon from something they just baked. The new shop is on the corner of Fourth and Washington. With walnut furniture, all simple and clean, but pops of mint green from the steel signs and chairs, it's certainly eye catching. Every table has a short clear vase with a few sprigs of baby's breath too. It's all sorts of happy and relaxed in this coffee shop. Completely at odds with how I'm feeling.

But this is the place Bethany picked. And so I'm here.

Blowing on the hot cup of caramel coffee, their flavor of the day, I think back to last night. Back to the moment I know I lost myself as I wait for Bethany to walk in the front door.

Is any pussy really that good?

His voice is deep and rough in my memory. I don't know if I've made it up, rethinking about that moment time after time in such a short period, or if he really sounded like that. There was a sense of awe, followed by a sense of loss that coated his words. I was a fiddle for him to play right then and there.

I thought after he took that first lick he'd lift his head and meet my stare to tell me, "No, it isn't that good." Swallowing thickly, I force down a sip of the coffee, not tasting it at all.

The way he treated me... I've never let a man treat me like that before. He's fucked me every way possible, but yesterday I let him touch me, not knowing if he respected me anymore. I'm ashamed I let Seth make me feel the way he did. The vulnerability is something I've never felt sexually with him and I hate it. I am ashamed and humiliated. I've never hated him before last night.

I've heard there's a thin line between love and hate, but damn, I never knew how true those words were.

What's worse is that I know it's the same for him. He has a mix of love and hate for me. I could *feel* it. It's all deserved.

That's why I never should have gotten on his desk. The way I craved him loving me… it's not possible for him to do that anymore. I should know better. That fleeting thought left me the moment his touch registered. I'm not interested in a hate fuck or being played with and treated as less than. If that's what he thinks this will be, I'll refuse, consequences be damned.

Seth's not apologetic; he's only demanding. It terrifies me most because I want to obey him. I want to do whatever he tells me because I am sorry. I hate what I did to him. I hate myself. He makes me hate myself.

Maybe a piece of me thinks he should be treating me like that… like I'm "less than."

"You okay?" Bethany's voice startles me and pulls me back to the present. Back to the hot mug I've got both hands wrapped around and the small ceramic plate of bite-size lemon cake squares.

"Yeah," I answer Bethany, setting the mug down and listening to the bells above the coffee shop door chime as an older man makes his way out. I didn't hear Bethany come in. "I didn't see you come in," I tell her.

As she pulls out the mint green metal stool on the other side of the table, the feet scrape against the floor and she simply stares at me.

There are at least six more patrons in the shop, a pair of maybe sixteen-year-olds—I don't even know if the two girls at the far end should be sipping on those lattes—and a few single adults scattered around the place. One's reading a book, others are scrolling through their phones and one man with white-as-snow hair is reading a newspaper. Bethany's got her back to all of them and her attention is centered on me.

"Sorry I'm late. I got into a little thing at home."

"Does it have to do with your sister?" I ask her in response, keeping my mind focused on the fact that everyone else has something going on in their life too. It's not all about me. It never will be. There's always someone else who needs help. It may seem inconsistent with logic, but that's what gets me through. Bethany nods and I'm quick to tell her, "I'm here for you, you know?" I put my hand over hers on the table and she takes it and squeezes it but then lets go as she sits back.

She seems to look right through me when she tells me, "It looks like you need someone more than me, to be honest." Bethany's blunt. She's always blunt. There's a kindness about the way she says things, but it cuts straight to the heart of the matter. She's a lot wiser than she appears, given how young she looks. She's been through hell and I know all about it. She came out fighting though.

We're silent as a waitress wearing a white apron with a mint green logo for Baked and Brewed stamped square on the front of it, places a cup of tea in front of Bethany.

"Thank you." Bethany smiles and then her dark red lips leave a smudge of lipstick behind on the white mug. That lipstick is what we first bonded over. "Lipstick courage" is what she responded when I complimented the shade. Later that night, she told me the name of it and I ordered a tube without thinking twice. There's a lot to be said about lipstick courage.

She stares at it a moment before tucking her brunette locks behind her ears.

"So, spill it," she requests.

It's been almost two weeks since I've seen Bethany and the last time we spoke in person things didn't go so well. It was my fault and I can still feel the distance between us. I hate it. Rubbing my hand down my face, I come to a certain realization. *Seems like I'm full of hate today.*

"I owe you an apology—"

"Stop it," she says, cutting me off. "You already apologized, for one." She swallows without looking back at me. It looks like she's lost weight since I've seen her. Meeting my gaze, she says, "Second, I know now."

"You know what?" I ask her, my fingers reaching for the ceramic mug.

Even with concealer under her eyes, I can tell she hasn't slept. Or maybe I'm just making it up, and I want to avoid talking about me, and move the conversation to her dilemma.

"That you know Seth," she confesses. She leans forward and says, "You knew him when I dragged you to his car. You could have told me." The last sentence she practically whispers and as she says it, I retract my hands from the table and move them to my lap.

"How do you know?"

"Jase." Bethany's answer is the name of her now-boyfriend. And Seth's employer. It's odd to think of Seth working for someone. He was never the type to take orders from anyone other than his father. He was bred to rule. It's simply who he is.

"What else did he tell you?" I question, my words coming out carefully. I feel a sick prickling along my skin. Bells chime above the café door and the sound steals my attention for only a fraction of a second. It's all too intense. Whenever Seth is involved, it's too intense.

"He told me not to tell you... so shhh, don't tell anyone I told you."

I roll my eyes as I comment, "As if I ever would," and try to take another sip of coffee. Again, I can't taste a thing.

All I can wonder is how much Jase knows. Did Seth tell him something? Did he tell him everything? I haven't told a soul. I can't even speak it out loud.

With a prick at the back of my eyes, I ask Bethany, my voice cracking, "Did he tell you what happened when I left? What made me leave?"

Her thick hair swishes as she sips her tea, never taking her eyes off of me. Maybe she's waiting for me to tell her, but there's not a chance in hell I will. I can't. I can't tell her about Cami.

With the silence separating us and adding an air of dread

to our corner of this little café, Bethany tells me, "He only said that you two were together back when you lived in California and then you left." I nod. I fled, I ran, I took off. *Left* seems like such an insignificant word.

She adds when I don't respond, "Jase said it looks like Seth followed you here."

"He didn't." I'm quick to correct her. Derrick told me he didn't. If he had, he would have come for me sooner. "He didn't come here for me."

Why does it hurt so much? Why does my heart twist and turn before going *thud*, *thud*, then pausing in my chest?

"Jase seems to think otherwise. I walked in on him and Carter talking about it."

The furrow of my brow works in time with my curiosity. My interest, and my concern piqued, I lean forward to question, "Why were they talking about it?"

Bethany shrugs, as if it's not a big deal. I don't want my name to be spoken by either of those men. The Cross brothers aren't known for generosity. They're brutal. Especially Carter. That sick prickling heats and makes my entire body burn with anxiety.

"Why did you leave?" she asks me and I'd be grateful for the change of subject away from the Cross brothers, had it been any other subject.

My finger plays at the rim of my mug, gliding along it as I inhale and exhale, forming the words in my mind first. I'm careful and deliberate with my answer when I say, "Things got hard and a bad thing happened to someone close to me." I peek up and Bethany's eyes are assessing. She's the best nurse at the Rockford Center, in my possibly biased opinion. It's one of the reasons I was drawn to her. She's damn good at what she does and she loves people in general. She loves making a difference and helping them. "Don't you dare treat me like one of the patients," I warn her.

Putting her hands up in the air, she protests that she never would. "If you don't want to tell me, that's okay." She resumes her position and cocks a brow at me before adding, "I won't push you."

Her reaction actually makes me huff a humorous laugh. "I've literally heard you tell that to patients."

She joins in my humor, giving me a genuine grin. It lightens the mood slightly, and I'm grateful for it. "I can't talk about it and get worked up. We're in a coffee shop, for fuck's sake. I don't even have mascara with me to touch up." I look her square in the eyes and see my friend again. The bond nearly physical between us, I joke, "I can't walk out of here with black streaks down my face."

She agrees, saying, "This place doesn't have a bathroom either. So no crying..." and then she persists in order to understand, "...but you left, you were emotional. The breakup was mutual?"

"Not really." My gut churns with my response.

"So you left him?" Fuck it hurts to hear her ask that. My heart agrees, stalling and refusing to resume beating until I respond. I nod and give a small *yeah*, ignoring the pain that claws at my gut.

There's no way in hell I'm going to be able to eat those lemon cake squares.

"And then he moved back but he's been here for a while and ..." I trail off and when Bethany doesn't say anything, I steel myself to confess the truth to her.

"And the night at the shopping center, our night out was the first time I'd seen him and spoken to him."

I'm surprised by the sorrow that worries Bethany's expression when she says, "And I just let you go with him. I'm sorry." Her voice cracks.

"You trusted him," I say to defend her and make sure that defense is audible. "It had to happen, Bethany. It was bound to. I'm happy you were with me when it did."

Her smile is weak, and the conversation pauses for a moment while she composes herself. "What did he say?" she asks once she's finally got a grip on her regret.

How do I tell her he didn't say a word to me? Again that shame rises at the fact I'd let a man get to me the way he did. More than that, protectiveness spreads through me. I find myself wanting to defend Seth. I don't want her to think of him like that. He wasn't always an asshole she'd hate this very second if she knew what transpired.

He was good.

I did this to him.

With a shuddering breath, I skip over the details of that night, only giving her the bare essentials: *He dropped me off and told me to meet him last night.*

Telling her what happened yesterday proves to be difficult too. I don't know how much of my perception is real. Was he cold to me like I remember? Or was he waiting to see what I'd do, like I was doing with him?

"It looks like more happened than just that, Laura," Bethany prods, when I try to gloss over it.

"The thing is, I'm not okay. Not emotionally. I keep finding myself back in that place I was when I left. It's like I'm grieving all over again."

"So this is about the bad thing that happened to someone close to you? Or leaving Seth?"

"I think both," I admit to her, truly unsure.

"An emotional state isn't linear." She reminds me of something I already know, and her eyes tell me she knows that I know.

"I know, but grief is supposed to be in stages and—"

She cuts me off, her voice pleading with me to understand. "Those stages misrepresent emotions. I just got into this with Aiden." She makes that last comment under her breath, fiddling with her napkin and then popping a lemon square in her mouth. Aiden is our boss at the Rockford Center. We don't always see eye to eye on things. It's good for the patients though. If one method isn't helping them, we have others.

"No, I know, and I agree with you. The stages are a depiction of the mental capacity to deal with shock and stressors that are too much to handle. Denial isn't an emotion, it's a coping mechanism. The stages are a timeline and they move in order and never in reverse because it's about coping, not about emotional ability." I stress the last line with the side of my hand hitting the table. "Yesterday, it felt like I was on a roller coaster, a scary one that I don't want to be on, and it kept moving back without warning, sending me down the same hill I ran from." The emotions, the wretched feeling I'm describing—it all creeps knowingly toward me again.

"It's not the stages of grief you're talking about. It's simply loss."

"It is," I admit quietly and close my eyes. "I'm feeling the loss all over again."

"Loss*es*," she says, stressing the plural, "and memories… they're chaotic, they come and go as they please with no patterns at times. They can be triggered."

"Well him being back in my life…" I start to tell her, grabbing hold of the reason, and therefore a semblance of control. "Seth saying…" I almost tell her *Babygirl*, but I don't want to give Bethany that much. It feels like a violation of what we have. "Seth saying my name…" I look her in the eyes only after I've spoken the last line of deception and continue,

"It's bringing back a lot of shit for me."

"That makes sense." She nods in understanding, and it helps. It makes such a difference just to feel understood. "You're wrecked. You look it, too."

"Well thanks, bestie," I joke and it makes us both ease into a short laugh. I have to sniffle, although I haven't cried and when I do, she continues.

"So you are emotional… in a negative way."

"Right."

"Were you afraid of what he'd do?"

"No, I was afraid of how he'd make me feel."

"How did he make you feel?" she asks.

"All sorts of ways."

"But did you get butterflies?" There's a note of optimism in her question.

I peek at her over my coffee, taking a large gulp and praying it gives me energy I desperately need. It's only lukewarm now. "Yeah, I got all sorts of butterflies." Every scene from yesterday washes over me. And even if he was… harder, harsher even, a heat I can't deny betrays my pride. "He…" I can't finish the statement without a blush warming my cheeks.

With wide eyes and an eager grin, Bethany reacts and says, "Oh my God, you're blushing. Since when do you blush?"

A laugh bubbles from my lips and I shake my head. I swear Seth will always give me butterflies. As if in response to that thought, my heart flutters that odd beat and I place my hand over the wild thing, trying to calm it.

"So …" Bethany presses.

"He thinks he can tell me what to do and I'll simply be his." For the second time today, I roll my eyes. It's followed by a smirk though as I add, "But he went down on me yesterday."

If it's possible, her eyes go even wider with this confession.

"He didn't get me off, though." I don't hide my disappointment.

Her response is comical and gets the attention of the older man with thin white hair as she exclaims, "Bastard!"

I smile into my coffee, sipping it. Even though it's not hot, it's delicious. "Yeah, he's a bastard. It's a little more serious than the way I'm saying it," I confess.

"The Cross brothers are always a little more serious."

"He's not a Cross brother."

"He's one of them. And they are more... intense. I understand that."

The air changes between us at the reminder of the occupation of our love interests, if I can even call Seth that anymore, making the lighthearted conversation steer back into the severity it will always claim.

"Sorry you didn't get off," Bethany says, trying to keep it light even though I know she can feel it too.

"Don't worry. I got myself off last night to spite him."

She laughs first and then I join in.

"Were you thinking of him?" she questions and even

though I don't laugh anymore, there's still the hint of a smile on my face when I nod. It's a sad smile though.

I thought of who he *used* to be. I don't tell her that.

Bethany chuckles and downs the rest of her tea. I don't laugh anymore. All the memories flicker back to me, ending with Cami and I have to set my mug down. Guilt worms its way up my throat, knowing I haven't told Bethany about Cami.

"You didn't tell me any of this in all the years we've been friends, you know?"

"I didn't tell anyone. I just wanted to forget."

"I get that. Doesn't look like you'll be able to forget now."

"I don't know how I'll get through it," I respond absently, not realizing how true the statement is until it's out there.

"You'll figure it out. You're a smart girl."

"Not when it comes to him." My heart tumbles at the very thought of him. Which reminds me... "I need to swing by the pharmacy and head out," I tell Bethany as I reach down to my satchel on the floor and search for my keys.

"Birth control?" she questions.

"Arrhythmia."

She blinks rapidly, a frown marring her face before picking up her teacup again. "I didn't know. I'm learning a lot about you today."

Worry and panic dance in the pit of my stomach. It's a short little number, but I know why. I'm afraid Bethany won't like me if she learns it all.

"I was diagnosed right before I left California. I didn't get the pills until after I'd moved away. You know how it is, I got busy with school and work. I didn't have any symptoms so I didn't refill my meds over the years. But I can feel it now."

"You shouldn't play around when it comes to heart problems." Bethany's comment sounds like something Cami said once. With a chill stretching lazily down my spine, my gaze catches a woman in the window the second I think of Cami. She's gone before I can see her fully. It was just a profile, but I swear it was Cami. She looked just like her.

"Hey, seriously," Bethany says and reaches out her hand, grabbing my right hand that's gripping the keys so tight I can feel the sharp edges digging into my fingers.

"Get your medicine and take it." She talks to me the way she does with the patients she cares so much about.

If I had any energy left, I'd tell her to knock it off. Instead I answer, "I know. I will."

"Promise?"

"I promise."

"You need to sleep too," she adds as she reaches for her purse and we both stand. It's the first time I get a full view of her getup. She looks like she's going out on a date in that black silk blouse and dark jeans. "You look like you didn't sleep at all."

"I took sweets last night to help." My comment stops her dead in her knee-high, black-leather-booted tracks. "It's just to help me sleep," I add to justify it. "I had a vial in my medicine cabinet from years ago when I first moved here."

"Sweets? Where the hell did you get sweets?" The surprise is just as evident in her voice as the contempt. As if I'm some sort of drug addict. She knows just as well as I do that plenty of our patients know exactly where to get all sorts of drugs. A lot of them self-medicate before they're even diagnosed.

"I had problems sleeping a while back," I explain to her, willing her to calm down. "A patient at the center said it would put me to sleep in an instant."

"You trusted the crazies?" Bethany says and eyes me like I'm a damn lunatic.

"No," I object, "although, eventually yes."

With her eyes closed, she looks like she's praying for mercy and patience. "I couldn't sleep; everyone could tell. Margret mentioned it every day. I tried melatonin, valerian—I even tried NyQuil for fuck's sake, until that wasn't working anymore. I tried everything I could get over the counter."

"You couldn't just go to the doctor's to get something?"

I shrug and say, "I tried everything; sweets were my last option. But it worked. It just lets you sleep."

"You know the men who sell it."

"It helps with addiction... you just sleep through the withdrawal." I try to justify it, but the truth is that the entire reason I resisted taking my patient's advice at first is because the sweets are dealt by the same men who sell everything else on street corners.

"If you say so," she says lowly and crosses her arms.

I'm quick to change the subject and ask, "When do you come back to work?"

"On Monday," she tells me and then counts the days. "Just four more days. I wish this weekend would be over already."

"I just switched my shift for tonight. I have today off, but I'll be working tomorrow and Sunday. I think I'm on for Monday too."

"Good, let's talk then?"

"Of course. I have to tell you what you missed at work too." I scrub at my tired eyes, careful of my mascara. "The world is changing quickly, isn't it?"

"Yeah it is. Go get your prescription."

"Love you," I tell Bethany. Gratitude swarms me knowing I have her as a true friend.

"Love you too," she tells me earnestly, pouting her lip just slightly and pulling me in for a tight hug.

I think about how I truly thought Cami would be the last person to ever say those words to me.

When I left, I knew Seth would never forgive me, because I couldn't even forgive myself. I bought a new place with the cash, I settled down and went to school. I didn't talk to a soul though. I was dying inside until I met Bethany.

Bethany hugs me tighter when I try to let go. She's stealing the method I use. Only two months ago, I did the same to her. I laugh a little, and she tells me again she loves me. It breaks me so I hold her back even tighter.

"Have hope," she whispers when I don't let go, bringing to mind the image of Seth and me together. I finally unwrap my arms from around her and close my eyes, telling her goodbye for now. When I open them, I swear I see that woman outside the window again. The coldness comes back and I swear she looks just like Cami from the back. Goosebumps travel quickly, gracing every inch of my skin.

"Laura?" Bethany's questioning voice rips me away from the woman and when I look again, she's gone.

"You okay?" My friend's tone is full of concern so I force a smile, ignoring the coldness that washes over me. "Yeah, yeah, I'm okay."

"Love you," I whisper when the chill comes back and I feel eyes on me once again, but I don't dare look to my right, toward the window.

"I love you too," Bethany tells me. My words weren't meant just for her though.

Chapter 5

Seth

Secrets get you killed in this business, but Laura doesn't have a damn thing to do with them. No one needs to know anything more about her other than what they can discover on their own.

"Who is she?" Jase still isn't letting up. He's asked me twice already today. Irritation swells in my chest as I release a silent exhale and school my expression.

My gaze stays glued to the clock behind the bar and the checklist repeats in my mind. It'll be different today with Laura.

I'll approach the situation with control. She needs it, but I need it more.

Last night I wasn't myself. Tonight, things will be different.

With the tick of another second gone by, I've forgotten all

about Jase and his fucking prying.

"You don't trust me?" he questions and an inkling of uneasiness creeps through me. The floor-to-ceiling windows in The Red Room offer little light as I grab my jacket. With rain threatening, the sky is darker than it should be for 3:00 p.m. The bar isn't open yet and I don't plan to be here when it does. When she has a day off, so do I. Simple as that.

I came for the meeting earlier, which is now over. All the men in charge of different operations were called to discuss the new developments overall. A management meeting, so to speak. Although the brothers never tell *all* of us *everything*. Trust and secrets go hand in hand.

The bar is quiet; it's just Jase and me left on this floor.

Slipping on my jacket, I finally face Jase, my back to the front door.

"I don't trust you?" I say, echoing his question back to him. Letting him see the ridiculousness of his statement. I don't trust easily, but I trust Jase. In those meetings, I know all the players and the information that is shared. If any details are omitted, I know why. I'm part of the inner circle and clearly a trusted member of his team. So yes, I trust him.

"It's hard to tell with you keeping secrets." He's pushing me, pressing me for information I've made clear I don't want to give. Worse, he's been digging for it anyhow.

"You know I trust you with my life," I speak under my breath and with an edge of warning, hating that I have to say the words out loud.

"It's not about that."

"What's it about then?"

"Secrets, Seth. It's about the fact that you're hiding something."

"I have this... alert..." I start to tell him and then second-guess myself, but not for long. "When I moved out here, I had a friend set it up. I had to know who was looking into me. So any time someone searches for me, digs into my past... I get an alert." I pause and note how quiet he is. "The searches were constant when I first started working with you. You know how it is. You need to know if someone's looking into you and what for. Fuck, I know Declan has the same or something similar active on every single one of the names associated with your family."

"Declan does?" Jase questions. He knows I'm close with his youngest brother. Closer to him than I am with any of the other Cross brothers. Jase narrows his eyes, like he hasn't caught on yet.

"He has one for Bethany too."

"When did he make one for Bethany?" he asks, truly unaware.

"I asked him to make one for her when you went to her house that first day."

"That first day?"

Instead of answering his question, of telling him how much

I had his back when it came to Bethany, I continue. "I made one for Laura too. I did it the second she left me. And I know you already know. I know when *anyone's* looking into her. I know you know who she is." I take a step forward, feeling the expensive suit jacket get tight around my shoulders. Cocking my brow and keeping the air between us as light as I can, I say, "So answer me this, who doesn't trust who?"

Jase's smirk is slow to form but it does, easily enough. The smirk and resistance for him to admit it bring that irritation back to the surface. I struggle to keep hold of my restraint. Maybe he can't feel the rage that's seeping into my remarks. I can though; the heat, the tightness in my chest. My jaw's clenched when I tell him, "I'm aware you already know the answers you're asking for. You've been looking into my background and then hers for weeks, yet you pretend like you don't know who she is?"

His gaze doesn't leave mine. Instead he stares back with a friendly look, although the intensity is at odds with the darkness in his eyes. "Don't get pissed. Since when are you this sensitive?"

"Sensitive?" I dare to bite back in what's nearly a snarl. "She's mine. And she doesn't concern you. I told you that. You don't need to look into her background."

"The fuck I don't." He puts on a façade that this is a relaxed conversation, but the tension grows around us by the half second. "Everything you do concerns me. Concerns all of us. You bring her in, whether you see it like that or not, and she's around us. She has access to the same information we do, how we act, where we are. I know her name, her résumé and credentials. I need to know more. *We* need to know more."

"Like what?" I question. "What do you need to know?"

"What does she want with you? And what do you want with her?" His questions are blunt and I break the hard stare between us to look back at the darkening sky behind us.

I answer him and my voice is low, barely speaking, "I don't know. I have no fucking clue and that's the truth."

"I'm going to need you to be careful with her."

"Why's that?" I say and turn back around to face him. Who the fuck is he to tell me what to do with her? "Is she a threat?" The menacing tone is more than apparent in my question.

"She's Bethany's friend." All emotion is restrained in Jase's voice. His answer is simply matter of fact. It takes me a long moment to realize what he's getting at.

He adds, "I don't need you interfering, messing with Bethany's head or getting to her."

Jase is my boss. He's powerful in ways I gave up any interest of being. So I glare back at him, listening to the thud in my chest and for the first time it feels the same as the first time I was arrested. With nothing else to do but wait, I slammed my fists over and over against the cinder block walls of the cell. *Thud. Thud. Thud.*

Licking my lower lip, I let my response linger on the tip of my tongue. Tasting it, debating it before finally looking Jase in the eyes to say, "She's always been mine and that's the only answer you need."

Taking a step back, I pivot on my back heel and turn my back to him. The soles of my polished oxfords groan as I turn on the waxed floors of the high-end bar. The bar I helped build. Carefully and quietly guiding Jase. I've done more than enough for them. They will not interfere. Or I'll make them regret it.

"At least you can admit that," Jase calls from behind and I pause. "You think it will stay that way?"

His question is met with a rise of anger. "What do you want from me?" I practically sneer the question as I whip around to face him and close the distance in an instant.

"To know what you're going to do. That's what I want, Seth."

"Leave her alone. She's mine and I'll take care of her how I want to."

Jase's clean-shaven jaw flexes at my defiance. With his dark jeans and light gray Henley he doesn't look like the man I know him to be. He's far too charming in his appearance. Far too laid back. Everything he does is intentional. Showing up to a meeting like this today, I knew he'd dispense bad news. It's all in delivery, in appearances. "Maybe I haven't been clear enough," I speak plainly, calmly, so that nothing can be misinterpreted. "I have no intention of sharing information about her. She's mine and she'll remain separate from the business. There are no exceptions."

"We have Marcus and Walsh both breathing down our necks. The batch of sweets that was stolen, our man murdered and even though we framed it like we planned it that way, we still don't know who did it." Jase pauses, his eyes searching my own.

"We've got problems, Seth. We can't find the stolen product. There's too much shit going on and too many unanswered questions. I don't like it." I nod, hearing the sincerity and concern. The bar is silent as the tension wanes. "I don't like you giving me even more questions and not answering them." He slips his hands into his pockets and I take a half step back. "She is an unknown variable. A distraction when you should be focused."

"I still have it for her," I admit to him.

"Have it?"

"Whatever it is that you get with a girl," I say.

Jase only nods, his dark eyes assessing. Wondering if I'm telling the truth. I'm wondering too. I know I'll tell him whatever he wants to hear so he'll back off.

"She's mine. She won't be a problem."

"You can guarantee that there won't be a single problem from this?" he asks although it's evident he already has an answer. Like he can sense the problems that will arise.

"She isn't a problem at all. More than that..." I pause as

I decide to give him the intel she gave me yesterday, even though I haven't read it all yet.

"There's a former resident at the center your girl works at—Delilah something—she has drawings of the places Marcus took her." His sharp eyes narrow at me, as if I've been keeping back information. He can fuck off with that.

"I'm going through the notebook but it's old. Laura's got more and she's bringing them today. I'm going through them, with Declan of course."

"Declan knows?" The fact that Declan's in on it has the hair that must've risen on the back of his neck falling back into place.

"Of course," I answer and give him a knowing look. "I talked to him before he left the meeting. He said not to transfer anything digitally. So I'll mark the pages I think may be worth a damn and give them to him."

"I'm curious to see if anything is relevant," Jase says easily, his shoulders relaxing for the first time since he's entered this damn bar.

"I know it's been tense with the shit Walsh and Marcus have been pulling. You don't have to question where my loyalty lies."

"It's not your loyalty I'm worried about."

"What is it then?" I ask him straight up. I need to put this to bed. Jase breathes in deeper, looking more tired than he has in a long damn time.

He shakes his head, which renews a surge of irritation. "There's something I haven't told you." He talks as he runs his hand down his face.

"Is that right?"

"We got a message from Marcus. Mailed with no return address, no postage or prints... It's his handwriting though. Something about Fletcher's right-hand man."

Hearing the name *Fletcher* sends a trail of unease down my spine.

"When?" I ask.

I'm answered with a question of his own. "Who's Fletcher?" He adds, "Yesterday. Just after you left."

"A dead man," I answer him. "Fletcher is long dead and in the ground. Can I see the note?" I ask, letting him know I remember where my place is in this organization. I'll make demands when it comes to Laura, but for business? It's up to them. I don't want to be in charge. I'm not interested anymore.

Reaching into his back pocket, he hands me the folded note:

Which will it be? Fletcher's right-hand man? Or Laura's father?

My stomach sinks and a cold wash of reality hits me hard. He knows. Marcus knows. Every hair stands upright on the back of my neck. Jase takes in every small change in my body language while reading that note. I know he does. The clenched jaw and difficulty staying still. I know he sees it all.

"What does it mean: *Which will it be?*" I ask him, repeating Marcus's question. It's harder and harder to breathe with this fucking tie on.

"I don't know but do you see why I'm concerned now?"

Chapter 6

Laura

The door doesn't open slowly, it's wrested open with intent and impatience.

The wind wails behind me, blowing past my shoulders and slipping into the sides of Seth's open jacket. It's a dark gray today, slim fit and accompanied with a black leather belt that probably costs more than the most expensive pair of shoes I own. I'm not cheap with my shoes either.

With a shiver tickling my shoulders, I pull the delicate cardigan tighter around me.

"You're early," he says as his tone and posture change, softening. The harsh grip he had on the door slowly slips and that makes my breath catch. That the sight of me could do that to him.

"Who did you think I was?" I ask, realizing his greeting was meant for someone else. "You were expecting someone?"

"No one... but you're never early." He's displaying more than a five o'clock shadow. He must not have shaved this morning. "Come in," he tells me, opening the door and holding it until I pass through, walking past him with each heavy and foreboding step. The roar of the fire in the living room straight ahead isn't the only sound I'm picking up on. There's also the steady thumping in my chest, harder than I've ever heard it.

Maybe it wishes to flutter and skip for the man behind me. The man who places his large hand at my hip, squeezing gently until he presses his hard chest to my back.

Thump, thump. The beat in my chest rages against my rib cage. If only I hadn't taken that pill, I know how wild my heart would be for him. Caged but uncontained.

He lowers his lips to the shell of my ear and I focus my sight on the fire; I barely noticed it yesterday. The flickers of yellow and orange flames slip through black stones in the modern fireplace. There's no wood, no fuel to speak of, but it roars intensely.

I can hear the moment he parts his lips, and my eyes instinctively close.

"Tell me why you're early, Babygirl," he whispers and the gentle tickle of his warm breath travels down my shoulder, both front and back. Eliciting a warning down my spine yet the goosebumps cause my nipples to perk and my core to heat as it travels down my front.

His hand moves to the front of my hip, curving against it.

"I didn't like the waiting," I answer him.

"No dress today?" he asks a little louder this time, less inviting, with less desire and more intrigue.

Instead of responding verbally, I shake my head. The crook of my neck must be more sensitive with his stubble rubbing against it as his thumb slips along the waistband of my favorite pair of blue jeans. I know it's more sensitive because even the shake of my head brings a spark of knowing as the strands of my hair brush along my heated skin.

I have to step out of his hold just to breathe. I take one step in my tan leather booties and look down at myself. Dark skinny jeans and a simple oversized cream cardigan covering a blush tank top. It's a more casual look than yesterday's. "I had a date before you," I comment, subconsciously teasing him.

I can see an alternate life in this instant. One where I'd never left him, one where we're still together and the vision gives me shivers. In my mind, I watch as I place my purse down on the coffee table, taunting him about my coffee date until I confessed it was only Bethany. And he smiles all the while, knowing I was toying with him, knowing he had me all to himself. I can practically hear the laugh I make when he jumps on the sofa in front of us I'd so casually laid on, giggling as he slips between my legs and nips my neck for teasing him.

Another life, a different one.

But I can *feel* it.

"I know you were with Bethany." Seth's response is all business and the moment he steps around me, not touching me, his absence gives me a different kind of coldness.

The one that lingers with this reality.

"You're tracking me?" I question him although it falls flat. Of course he is. He doesn't even bother to answer. "Spies?"

Again, I get no answer. He simply walks to the kitchen, a small one at that for the large, open-concept main floor.

I listen as he pours the drinks, noting how there's no art on the wall except a single piece. It's a black-and-white modern artwork, very sexual with the silhouette of a woman's figure straddling over a chair. It's so close up, and the contrast muted, that at first glance, it's only lines. Abstract art with no meaning. But then I can see what it is clearly, because I remember the day he took that photo of me.

My breath leaves me and I lose my composure the second I recognize it.

"I thought about getting rid of it." Seth's confession comes from the kitchen and rips me away from the memory I long to go back to.

His dark blue eyes pierce through mine, holding me captive as he lifts two glasses off the counter. "Sit," he commands and caught in his trance, I move. I even place my purse right where I had in the fucked-up reality my head had conjured a moment ago. Instead of tossing it playfully, I set it down methodically and sit back against the gray sofa, gripping the edge of it and trying to hold on to my sanity.

"I bought it just before you left. Before that night. It hadn't come in yet, but I got it for you." My nails dig into the sofa, and suddenly the fire raging across from me seems too much. The heat is too overwhelming.

"I don't like you bringing that day up," I'm quick to tell him, feeling the anxiousness roll inside of me.

It's quiet for a long moment. With my eyes closed all I can hear is the fire, followed by the sound of our glasses being set on the slick all-black coffee table and then of Seth drinking from his.

"It stayed covered for... it had to have been three or four years. I'd forgotten about it until I unwrapped it along with everything else that was shipped here."

The sofa dips with his weight as Seth sits on the opposite end of the sofa.

"It stayed on the floor, leaning against the wall with its back showing, for a long time."

I finally peek up at him through my thick lashes and dare to question, "Why? Why not get rid of it?"

"It was a reminder of what I lost. Those memories can give a man a lot of power. And motivation."

I only nod my head before reaching for the glass. It's cold and the beads of condensation are welcome when I grip it.

With my eyes on the painting, hung up to the right of the fireplace, not centered above it, I take a sip of the vodka and soda.

"Do you like it?" Seth asks easily. "I thought about taking it down before you came, but I wanted to know if you remembered."

"My birthday," I say, giving him the information he'd need to know that I recall exactly when the photo was taken. "I remember... I love it."

His exhale is easy as he takes another drink. I watch as he swallows and he only glances at the art piece before looking into my gaze. "I thought you'd like it for the bedroom," he admits and a flash of emotion plays in his eyes. He breathes out like his thought is funny before downing the drink and abruptly standing. "I couldn't throw it out," he says with his back to me as he walks to the kitchen. "I couldn't touch it."

As he makes himself another drink, not bothering with ice and simply adding more whiskey to his tumbler, I hold on to mine. Feeling the diamond pattern carved into the heavy lead crystal.

Even with the cool drink, my throat feels dry and tight.

"A painter hung it while I was out. He thought I meant to hang it. And I couldn't touch it to take it down."

"I'm sorry it bothered you," I speak and my voice cracks before I down my own drink.

He's there, placing his glass on the coffee table and

holding his hand out for mine when I finish.

On his walk to the kitchen, he doesn't respond to my comment other than to say, "Everything happens for a reason, doesn't it?" Damn, do I hate that response right now.

He can't hear my faint *yeah* from where I am as he stands in the kitchen. After handing me my glass, this one full to the brim rather than only halfway, Seth takes off his jacket and unbuttons his shirt.

My pulse quickens when he continues to undress himself until he's only in his suit pants. I watch as he takes off his shoes, slipping his socks into them like he used to do. His muscles ripple with power and precision. The fire emphasizes every dip I crave to touch.

He's older, his shoulders broader, his body more muscular and toned. I can't take my eyes from his taut skin and the way his body moves. The warmth from the fire is nothing compared to the heat that kisses every inch of my skin while watching him.

"Getting comfortable?" I ask him. Again, nearly teasing. He looks up at me first, dropping his polished black shoes to the ground next to the fireplace, closest to the hall we walked down last time. With an asymmetric smirk, he comments, "You didn't change, did you?"

"So much of me has changed," I answer him without thinking about what to say. Without forming a list in my head of every aspect of my life that doesn't at all resemble who I used to be.

With my manicured nail tapping along the glass, I speak up, telling him something I decided I had to confess hours ago when I was thinking about how tonight would play out. "I made excuses for you today." My hardened voice and the confidence in it, makes him hesitate before he takes back his seat in nothing but those pants. Everything about him reads powerful and dominant. "I blamed myself for your actions."

With his legs spread, he leans back with his drink, his gaze moving between me and the fire, but landing on me in the end when I don't take my gaze from his.

He sips his drink rather than responding and I tell him, "I won't do that."

"Do what?"

"Blame myself."

"Then don't," he answers easily enough. My bottom lip wavers until I take another unsteady sip and close my eyes.

"What you did yesterday..." I trail off as I remember how I felt on his desk and the wave is an onslaught to my confidence.

The sound of him leaning forward forces my eyes to open wide, the sofa groaning, before I feel him closer to me.

"What did I do that was so wrong that you felt the need to make an excuse?" His question holds a taste of menace.

"You wanted to humiliate me."

"The fuck I did."

Anger rolls off of me in harsh and unforgiving waves. "Yes

you did, you acted like I—"

"I wanted you to know how I coped with you leaving; I wanted you to *feel* it." His words are rushed, pushed through gritted teeth. Clearly he's referring to the note. Which is an entirely different matter.

"You had me lay on that desk so you could prove your power over me." I know that's why. I know it is and I can't even breathe as I wait for him to deny it. "To demean me."

He shakes his head. "I wanted to taste you again, that's not humiliating."

"Could any pussy taste that good?" I mock him, feeling that humiliation once again.

"I didn't say it like that," he speaks clearly, sucking on a piece of melted ice between his teeth. He lets it fall back to his empty glass. It pisses me off how he hides the emotion he clearly had a moment ago.

"How is that not humiliating?"

"I wasn't aiming for humiliation," he admits. His gaze unwavering, he fixes me with a calm and dominating stare, not moving. "I was just telling the truth."

Not knowing how to respond, I move to the next item on the list. "Worse, you wanted me to feel bad about the note. You wanted me to feel guilty."

"You are guilty. You're the one who left." Again his answer is matter of fact. *Guilty.* I can't stand it. I can't stand the word. As if all of this is my fault. The control he has makes me lose what little of it I have.

"You're the one who didn't change!"

"You're the one who wanted me to change."

I don't know how I'm able to stand, my legs feel so weak. But I do, as quickly as I can, reaching for my purse to leave.

"Sit down." Seth's authority makes me pause.

"Everything hurts," I admit to him. "I can't be here without hurting. I can't see you without hurting."

When I look down at Seth, through the glaze of tears I hold back, I feel a wave of fear and desire mix. It swirls through my blood and I lose my own thoughts, my concentration. I lose everything to the way he looks at me.

"You're going to do what I say, because you want to... and there's no humiliation in that."

"I never said I wanted to."

"You're here early, Babygirl. You didn't have to say it." *Babygirl.* The desire is immediate and warms everything. He stands and steps forward, taking my purse and tossing it back down onto the table. My breath comes faster, my head feeling lighter.

He whispers, his lips only inches from mine. "Know that I want you, too, because I stare at that painting every day, wishing I could go back to that moment."

Taking his seat again, he repeats, "Sit down." And this time I do.

"You're going to obey me, because it will take that pain

and that guilt away."

I close my eyes slowly, careful to hold back any tears and calm myself down. "Not everything. I don't agree to doing whatever you say."

His answer is spoken with confidence. "You will. You're better at it now than you were back then."

"Don't do that," I say and glare at him. Feeling a wash of anxiousness.

"What?"

"Bring up the past." My heart thrashes in my chest, as if it's at war.

"You will do what I say, and I will be mindful of what I tell you to do and how I say it." Seth's proposition eases a burning pain that's quick to ignite every time I think back to what used to be.

As he waits for me to agree or to continue this fight, I consider what he said... the *guilt*.

God it hurts.

"I just want it to stop," I whisper, feeling the pricks at the back of my eyes.

"Want what to stop?"

"The guilt." Admitting it out loud brings a torrent of emotion.

"Strip down," Seth commands me, not responding to the emotion I'm clearly displaying. Not giving it any credence in the least. He doesn't try to comfort me, and damn my desire,

I want him to. I want to crawl into his lap, I want to beg for his forgiveness.

"Strip down to nothing," he demands in a calm and controlled voice. His glass clinks as he sets it on the table and then leans back, his large hands clasped as he waits for me to obey.

The discord of what I want, what I need, who I am and what I used to be rips apart who I know myself to be.

The crackle of the fire feels like a whip against my bare shoulder when I slip off the cardigan. It glides slowly down my skin and I feel it settle against my shoes into a puddle of fabric. The blush tank top is harder to take off. Not physically, but emotionally.

I'm so aware of the fear. I feel like nothing when he looks at me. But I want to feel like everything. I have to close my eyes to do it, to pull the tank top over my head and do as he wishes.

"Look at me," he says and it's as though his command physically strikes me. Inhaling and exhaling, controlling my breathing and holding on to the fact that I refuse to leave here without trying, I do it.

I don't know what I'm trying to do though. Even as I kick off my shoes and my jeans are stripped from me by my own hands, I don't know what I want.

As if reading my mind, Seth sits up straighter on the sofa, his erection evident against his suit pants. The fabric is tighter along his length, outlining it and he rubs it once before telling me, "You want to feel better and so do I."

I do.

God, I desperately do.

His eyes darken, the fire flickering within them. "Your bra and then your underwear."

I do as he says. The clasp easily parting and the sound of my bra hitting the floor is louder than it ought to be.

When I step out of my underwear, I'm a half step closer to him, but before I give in and let go, I make him promise me something. "Tell me you don't just want to embarrass me and toy with me."

I can't explain why it means so much to me. But I need to believe it's more than that for him.

"I want to toy with you, yes. But you were never embarrassed before. Humiliating you doesn't get me off." His gaze roams down my body, his lips parted as he exhales. "I want you to listen to me. That's what it boils down to. I just want you to listen to me."

He has to look away, back to his drink that's empty when he tells me the last bit. *He just wants me to listen.* He stalks off, leaving me naked as he goes back to the kitchen, feeling miles away.

He thinks if I'd listened things would be different. The whispered explanation brings a new hurt and new guilt.

"Stop it. Stop thinking. Do what I tell you to." Seth reappears without a glass in hand.

So many years have passed but I still want to please him. I wonder if that will ever change.

"What do you want?" I ask him as calmly as I can. I can still remember the first time I was conscious of that desire. I wanted to please him.

As I watch Seth push the coffee table toward the fireplace, I recall that night.

It was at the old bar, the one my father used to leave me at all the time growing up. And it was just after his funeral. Derrick called me "Babygirl." *Derrick* did. I knew him to be a friend of Seth's. I even liked him. He would look out for me. It was he who welcomed me into the bar to wait for Seth.

I wasn't *Derrick's* Babygirl and my reaction must've told him as much. "Oh," he'd said with a smile. "You want that just for Seth, don't you?" His question wasn't teasing, only knowing. At that moment Seth walked in. Everything was chaotic back then, after Vito was killed. Seth's father was in charge; he hadn't been murdered yet in the war for that territory. Still, Seth was needed and commanded more than anyone else. It was like his father was grooming him.

Seth came in and needed a beer. Looking distracted, he kept heading to the bar but man after man stopped him. They needed him and he gave them the time they wanted. Those days, he still walked me to and from home at night. Just me, not letting anyone come with us. He made time for me. We hadn't even kissed, but he liked to touch me when I was around him. He always held my hand, touched my back; he'd run his finger down the back of my neck absently when Derrick talked to him. He hadn't done a damn thing sexual, but it felt like everything to me that he wanted me near enough to touch. He never made the first move though. Not that quickly after things changed, and not for months later.

I was no one when it came down to it, and he was going to be everything. I could feel it.

I would only be his Babygirl. With that thought in mind, I got a beer for him and put it in his hand as he talked. I wanted to please him, and I had. The way he looked at me, ignoring whoever had been speaking, did something inside of me.

I can feel the same stare now as Seth rounds me years later. He did exactly what I expected him to; he ruled, like the king he was meant to be.

Myself, on the other hand? I wasn't even strong enough to be his Babygirl.

"Did you sleep last night?" Seth's question brings my gaze to his, makes me focus on the present.

"Some," I answer honestly. He doesn't look in my eyes when he stands in front of me, because he's focused on my chest. It's not until his hot touch grips my right breast and my head falls back just slightly that his gaze reaches mine. With his thumb and forefinger, he rolls my nipple and I have to bite down on my bottom lip to keep from moaning out at the sharp pleasure.

"Did you touch yourself?"

"What?" My eyes widen as I betray myself. I know it's obvious. I've never been a good liar.

"You used to. You used to punish me with it too. Taking care of yourself and letting me know you had." He squeezes my left nipple harder than the right, causing me to lean forward until he pulls back. A wave of pleasure rushes through me, stirring in my belly when he releases his hold.

With my lips parted, I breathe in deeply, sucking in a breath when Seth does it again. Both of my nipples, both at once.

"Look at me," he commands and I do. Staring into the depths of his eyes as he rolls my nipples between his deft fingers. "Did it feel like this?"

"No," I answer immediately.

"Did you think of me?" he questions and I hate to admit it, I hate knowing I thought of the good moments with him. All the nights I gave myself completely to him.

I can't answer verbally, so I only nod.

He plucks them both at once and the hot sensation is linked to my clit. I nearly stumble from the pleasure.

"You're a bad submissive." Hearing him say submissive forces a smile to grace my lips. He turns away from me, moving to a chest that sits by the fireplace, just under the painting hung on the wall. Standing there, watching his muscular shoulders, I dare to toy with him. "You're not my dom."

"That's where you're wrong, Babygirl." He stands up as he

breathes out, holding a leather paddle in his right hand and slapping it down on the palm of his left. I instantly clench, feeling how hot and wet I am already. His burning gaze heats my own as he tells me, making his way to me, "Your body knows it. One day you'll get it through that thick skull of yours."

My body's tense with the sight of the paddle. Braided strips of black leather are wrapped around the entire length. His gaze is heated when he tells me to bend over and grab the back of the sofa, but not to rest my knees on the cushion.

It's awkward to stand like this, since I'm so short. I listen though, knowing full well he plans to use that paddle on my ass.

Thwack! He doesn't waste any time. The moment both my hands grip the sofa, he spanks me with it. The burning pain ricochets through me, starting at my right ass cheek, and I swear, by the time it returns to my core, it feels like heaven. The pain and pleasure are braided together as tightly as the leather.

Seth takes his time, kicking my clothes out of the way before touching his palm to my heated flesh. He squeezes my sore cheeks and in return, I moan a strangled sound. Leaning my forehead against his sofa, I try to keep still when he smacks my ass with the paddle again.

"Three times," he tells me before quickly bringing the paddle down again. The pain is more intense this time, the strike unexpected and I scream out in brutal agony as my legs buckle and beg me to brace myself on the cushion of the sofa. I don't though; balancing on the balls of my feet, I make sure I stay where I am. My face is contorted until the leather slips through my thighs, brushing against my clit. He rocks it, letting the pleasure build as he wraps my hair around his other wrist and pulls back so I can no longer rest on the back of the sofa. "No more touching yourself or all of your punishments will be as hard as that last one was. Understood?"

With my eyes closed, I agree. "Understood."

He's never been like this before. Never with me. The control, the patience, I know that is his nature, but this is so much... more.

He releases me too quickly, far before I'm ready to let go and fall from the cliff of my release. The pleasure wanes, the pain of my punishment returns and I find myself needy and turning around to see what he's doing.

I turn at the perfect moment, seeing him in all his naked glory as he kicks off his pants, the last remaining garment covering him from me. Every inch of his body reminds me of Adonis. He is sex personified. My inhale is sharp when he turns around, and his gaze is narrowed as he tsks me.

"I didn't say you could turn around," he scolds me, although the lust in his voice and the desire in his gaze are so clear, it feels nothing like a reprimand.

"You didn't say I couldn't," I argue lustily, setting the side of my head back down, taking him in and letting him know just how much I want him. How much I need him.

"Keep your eyes on me then," he speaks calmly as he walks behind me. With one hand stroking himself, I can already see the beads of precum at his velvety head. "How many men did you fuck?" he asks and I blink twice, rapidly.

Hesitating, he urges me to answer with his hand splayed on my lower back. He brings his knuckles up my back to my shoulders and then back down.

"It's been eight years," I tell him as if that's an answer. His erection presses between my folds, thick and hard as he rocks against me. The groan he lets out, *fuck*, I could cum to that sound any night. He bends down when I close my eyes, enjoying the sensation. With his hips pressing against my ass and his cock nudging my clit, the pleasure builds again.

"Open your eyes," he commands, his stubble brushing against my shoulder and I watch as he closes his own and kisses the crook of my neck.

I miss this.

I have dreamed of him doing just this for years.

"How many men did you fuck?" he asks me again, this time in a whisper, his warm breath sending shivers of want down my body.

"Many," I answer him and remember how none of them compared. How at first it was hard trying to find someone who I could hide my past from, but share my present. Then it was simply about trying to find anyone who could fill a portion of the void.

Seth chuckles, deep and rough, his chest vibrating against my back. "You're my little slut now." His comment only makes me hotter for him.

"So tell me, my little whore, how many pricks got to play with what's mine?"

"Not *whore*," I argue, barely able to get out the words as I shake my head against the fabric and practically moan my reply. "Slut." I repeat the word, clenching around nothing again and imagining him inside of me.

"My little slut," he whispers and the feel of his warm breath along my skin brings the pleasure closer to the surface, closer to igniting all of me.

"How many pricks got to play with what's mine?"

I stare back at him, unable to answer as he grips my hair at the back of my neck, still rocking his hips, still playing with me. Still wanting me.

I can't speak as the pleasure builds.

"You're not allowed to cum until I know how many times to deprive you. I need to know how many times."

Defiantly, my back arches as my orgasm rips through me.

Seth stills behind me and I clench against the shaft of his cock. It's a blinding pleasure. I can barely breathe.

"Ever defying me aren't you, Babygirl?" Seth scolds me, taking more of my hair in his fist and pulling back when I look away from him. The tight grip sends a stinging pain along my skin, but it only heightens the pleasure.

"Does thinking about being punished get you off?" he asks.

"Thinking that you cared who I fucked... that gets me off." The admission comes out willingly, easily.

Seth King still wants me. He wants me to be his. That realization comes with one of my own. I want to be his. I've been waiting to be his again.

Chapter 7

Seth

It takes every ounce of control not to cum with her. Her cheeks are flushed, as pink as her ass where the braided marks have left impressions on her skin. She's everything I remember and more.

The memories don't do her justice.

Knowing how easy it was to get her off drives me insane. How much she still wants me, enough to let this strong woman, want to be called my little slut... fuck, I could cum without even entering her.

The fire at my back is nothing compared to the crackling air between us.

"How many?" I question her. Ignoring the screaming rage in my head, demanding she be punished for not listening to me. She wasn't allowed to get off until I'd punished her for each and every one.

"Not enough," she answers, her eyes closing but the moment I pull back on her hair, just slightly, just enough to control her, her baby blues sink into mine and she adds, "I tried to fuck the memories of you out of me."

"Did it work?" With the question lingering between us, my heart slams against my chest, racing to get out of me.

"Not even for a single moment," she whispers, and the pain creeps back into the depths of her gaze. The longing, the need.

I slam into her, my plan, my control, completely gone. I can't restrain the need to have her, to take her and make her mine like she ought to be in this moment.

Deep inside of her, to the hilt, I watch as her neck arches, her head falling back with a wretched scream of pleasure. Her cunt spasms around my length, the warmth and heat stroking a desire that forces my balls to draw up. I could let go just like this. Gripping her hair, feeling her curves, hearing her screams and buried deep inside her as she orgasms from the forceful thrust.

A cold sweat breaks out along my skin, every inch of it covered, trembling with the need to move. I wait, letting her adjust, refusing to give in to the baser need.

A second passes, Laura's body sags and that's my cue to piston my hips. Control and desperation are at war with one another as I fuck her with complete possession. Pulling her hair back, I whisper along the crook of her neck, "You are mine," never pausing the steady pace of my thrusts.

The sound of it, of my hips meeting her ass, mixes with the short moans that slip out of her parted lips every time I sink inside of her.

This. I have missed this dearly. I ravage her and nothing has given me more meaning in my life. Harder, faster; I fuck her more and more ruthlessly until Laura's grip slips, unable to hold on. Letting go of her hair and wrapping my arm around her waist, I shove her to her knees, mine resting just on the outside of hers on the sofa cushion. I don't miss a beat as she thrashes under me, screaming louder and with a frenzy she can't control. Even the sound of her nails scratching against the sofa fuels me.

She screams my name. Mine.

"You're mine," I remind her. Whispering the heated truth. "You're mine."

"Seth," she begs me, but I haven't a clue what for. She could beg for anything now, and I wouldn't stop. I can't. But when I'd finished, I could have promised her the world, just to keep her under me.

"You're mine." The savage words are gritted between my teeth before I rake them down her slender neck. Her lips never close, her screams of pleasures and heavy breathing never pause. Her nails claw down my thigh as she reaches behind her and the hint of pain urges me to fuck her harder and faster.

She's lost in the pleasure, limp and sated, but on the verge of cumming yet again. Her body trembles with the need but her glazed gaze and whispered pleas prove to me she's uncertain if she can take it.

"Take it, Babygirl. You. Are. Mine. Take it." I can't stop. Not yet.

I can't let go. Not until she admits it.

I won't tell her to though. I won't command her to acknowledge what I deserve to hear.

With both of my hands gripping her hips to keep her upright, she takes it all. For over an hour, I refrain, letting her cum time and time again.

I don't let go until Laura screams out, pulsing around me, "I'm yours."

She's limp on the sofa, her thighs pressed together as she turns from side to side. Her skin is a beautiful pink, her hair a messy halo. She's a vision of beauty and nothing less. "Mmm," she moans, biting her bottom lip as she rolls onto her side again, swaying her legs and moving her hands to rest between her thighs.

"Did I break you, Babygirl?" I ask her.

"Hmm," she breathes, her blue eyes searching for mine when she finally looks up. "Seth? You ruined me long ago."

Her body trembles, even as she clings to me when I lean down to pick her up. The evidence of her giving into me surrounds us. From the damp spot where she was just laying, to the clothes strewn around the room.

Her cheek rests on my shoulder as I walk down the hallway, to my bedroom. "You'll stay here tonight." The statement seems to wake her, to make her more sober than she's been for the last hour that I've had her at my mercy. Her grip slips on me, but I hold her just the same.

With a short intake of breath and a hesitancy in her touch, I expect her to protest. She doesn't though. She doesn't do a damn thing when I pull my sheets back, slipping her into the large four post bed and then covering her small body.

"Sleep." I give her the command and her wide doe eyes stare up at me. The look in them is resistant and questioning, but she's quiet.

It's not until I'm leaving the room, until my back is to her and my hand is on the doorknob to close it behind me that she speaks up.

"Seth," she calls out.

"Yes?" I question her, waiting for her defiance so I can shut it down. She will stay here tonight and any other night I want. *She's mine.*

"The other notebooks... I brought the photocopies in a

file box." Her voice is clear and I debate whether or not she'll even be able to sleep until she blinks. It's slow, sleep longing to keep her eyes shut. When I don't respond, I simply watch her figure, the moonlight playing with the shadows along her curves under the white comforter. *My gorgeous girl.* Then she adds, "It's in my trunk."

"I'll get them. Go to sleep."

She doesn't agree. She doesn't protest either. She simply watches me as I close the door, making a mental note to reward her in the morning.

Chapter 8

Laura

Even though I'm not there anymore, I can't help thinking: it's been a long damn time since I've woken up in someone else's bed. I like to leave in the middle of the night, if I bother staying after a round in the sheets with a man. I only remember staying with one of the guys I'd actually slept with in his bed till morning.

And I never bring them back here. Never. My loft is my safe place.

So as the hot water sprays against my skin, feeling especially brutal against my ass, I think there's only been one other time, one other guy who I've laid in bed next to and slept till morning.

I don't even remember that poor guy's name. It was a

decent night, but I only stayed because I'd come off a long shift before the date. It was just fine. Everything about every other guy is always... just fine.

Turning around to wash away the soap that's lathered on my front, I open my mouth and drink some of the hot water. The steam fills the stall and I stare absently at the grayish-blue subway tile. I thought about objecting more than I thought about sleeping when Seth was there, staring at me expectantly. The moment the door closed and I closed my eyes, all I could smell was him. That woodsy, masculine scent that reminds me of home.

Nothing reminds me of home... nothing but Seth.

All I could smell was him; all I could feel were his hands on me, his cock inside of me. *Fuck*, even now as I wash myself, my hands reach lower and I swear I can still feel him pulsing inside of me.

Even with the heat surrounding me, I shiver. Loving the way it feels, loving the memory of it.

The moment I closed my eyes last night and let myself be consumed by the remnants of Seth, I fell deep asleep. It was dreamless, but peaceful. I haven't slept like that in years.

Ding-dong.

The doorbell sounds loudly in my bathroom. The loft is small enough to hear that thing from any corner of my home.

I'm quick to turn off the spray and dry off haphazardly before throwing on a cotton bathrobe. I'm nowhere near presentable, but I can at least peek through the peephole. As I walk, I catch a glimpse of the large clock on the wall in my living room. It's a farmhouse design, galvanized silver and oval with barn wood behind the moving hands. It's not even noon yet. I've been home for nearly two hours since Seth and I parted, him to work, whatever that might be.

It reminds me of what else I was thinking about in the shower.

It's been a long damn time since I've slept in a man's bed. An even longer time since I've woken up to an early morning lazy fuck. With the tingling sensation still ringing along my skin, I open the door for the delivery woman.

With her hair pulled into a tight bun and a ruby red smile, she asks my name and makes me sign before handing me a long rectangular white box.

I'm glad it's a woman, since my robe slips open just slightly as I sign. She can't see anything, but still.

Kicking the door shut behind me, I wonder what's in the box. There's a single ribbon, satin and dark red, in the center of it. It's easy enough to untie. There's no note, no sender information. Only my name. Not even an address.

At the realization, I turn back to look at my front door. Questions are ringing in my head. I'm sure she's long gone, so instead of chasing her, I merely purse my lips and open the box.

Long-stemmed flowers. Their soft floral scent hits my senses just as quickly as the smile on my face and warmth up my chest.

With my bare feet padding on the floor and water still dripping from the tips of my hair, I trace the petals of the blush buttercup ranunculus and the white anemones. It's a full bouquet and given that it's fall, I imagine it wasn't cheap.

Grabbing the step stool so I can reach the top shelf, I take out my expensive vase, not the basic clear ones that are on the bottom shelf.

I cut each stem, remembering when Seth gave me a similar bouquet. It was our first year anniversary. I think it's the first real gift he ever got me. Technically we never gave ourselves a date. But every year, on the date of our first kiss and our first night together, Seth gave me a bouquet, and this one was the first. These flowers and these colors. Much smaller and not quite as fancy as these are, but the same flowers.

I can't believe he remembered. Men never remember details like this.

I leave the vase in the center of my coffee table, and when I'm done cleaning up, I lie down on the sofa, still in my robe, and question everything I thought up until yesterday.

What am I doing? The question nags at me. More importantly, I hear Seth's voice in my head from only weeks ago, asking me how I thought this would end.

Chapter 9

Seth

"The notebooks are mostly ramblings. But there are drawings of where Marcus took her." The woman, Delilah, likes to sketch. I wondered how accurate they were until I drove past one of the streets she referred to. She'd drawn a park, specifically Lincoln Park. It was the first place she'd met Marcus according to the notebooks. It's the place that started it all. It was like she'd taken a photograph. It was that detailed and that accurate.

"Drawings?" Jase questions from where he sits behind his desk. Declan's occupying the chair next to mine, on the opposite side of the desk. I answer, although Declan knows just as well as I do.

"Some in New York, where she's from, but she came down

here years ago for a case and that's apparently where she met Marcus. She drew the locations."

"Maybe it's something she did back when she was a lawyer?" Jase surmises.

"More like she learned it from a cop," Declan speaks up and steals our attention. "I've been going through Walsh's computer. He's uploaded his old cases and in his files, he drew the sites. Quick sketches."

"Maybe she learned it from him? She was a lawyer, right? Did they work a case together?" This is the first time Declan's telling me this.

"Could be," he says then shrugs and sits back in his seat. The leather groans and with the turn of the clouds, Jase's office darkens. He has to get up to turn on the lights as the day shifts to night behind the large window to the back of him.

"She was with Walsh and Marcus. She has information on both of them. She met Walsh first."

Sitting forward, I nod as I clasp my hands in my lap. My thumb runs along my knuckles as I tell him, "There's a lot in these notebooks that could be useful if the information is still accurate. Like how Walsh used PO Boxes to communicate with informants. He used them to send her letters too. It's a safe place for an information exchange. Or at least he considers it to be since they're purchased and paid for by an LLC that's run through the Cayman Islands."

"Our surveillance shows he's still using them," Declan adds.

"Good, let's see who he's still talking to and if there's something sensitive we can use to our advantage."

It shouldn't surprise me that the information Laura gave us is already paying off.

"Do you think he's still seeing her?" Jase asks and I look to my right, waiting for Declan to speak up. I gave him the latter half and the first one I'd already read, and I took the earlier portion. "Declan has the most recent entries of her diaries."

"It appears she still occasionally has contact with him and she's made it clear she isn't over him. What they went through, it certainly changed her career path and mental state."

"An up-and-coming lawyer, to an in-and-out resident at a mental institution... I'd say so."

"Anything in there about Walsh?" Jase questions.

I thumb through the pile of papers in front of me as I shake my head. "Not anything after the first year of entries. She hasn't written anything about him recently."

"It's possible that she may not know Walsh is looking for her?" Jase says and I can feel the steady tapping of the heel of his foot under the desk. His ass is riding on this just as much as mine is.

"Is he?" Declan asks.

"He mentioned her at the very least. So she's on his mind."

"As far as we know," Declan answers, "he hasn't contacted her."

I add in my thoughts. "It's odd that he hasn't. He's

obviously not over what happened years ago and it involves her. She was a key piece in whatever happened in New York that led to him leaving the FBI."

"He has to know where she is. It's only a matter of time before he contacts her." Jase sounds confident and I'm confident he will as well.

"Maybe he's waiting for something," I suggest and that gets Jase's gaze pinned to mine, eager to know what I think after reading the diary entries.

"For what?"

"For Marcus to be out of the way." Declan nods in agreement with me.

It's quiet for a moment, the room still and the only sound the click of the HVAC system and the low hum of air as the heater's engaged.

"We wanted something to barter with. I don't think information on Delilah is enough. If it was, Walsh would be there already."

"We could kidnap her, trade her for it, but I don't see that ending well. And we don't know where she is right now. She's a ghost until she needs help and meds. Should be soon though."

"He'd lie, get her back, then put us away with a copy of the recordings he didn't give us."

"Agreed. We have to play it another way." Jase sits back in his seat, staring past us and at nothing in particular. "If things go wrong, we take her. As an insurance policy. But for now, we play it differently."

"At least we know our next move, steps ahead." Declan is the least tense of the three of us. "I'll have the team keep eyes on her. Just in case."

"Good." Jase still doesn't look at either of us. He's thinking. The wheels spinning, all the possible moves playing out. I can see his thoughts clearly, easily reading him after all the years of getting to know him.

"What are you thinking?" I ask him when the tapping of his foot stops.

"We have two things on Marcus."

I name the two, completing his thought. "A list of men who work for him that we've been following and journals of a woman he seems to have affection for. Although we don't have her location. She goes off the grid, but always goes back to the Rockford Center eventually."

"As well as the knowledge that she's been seeing Marcus," Declan adds and Jase nods, the two sharing a look. "The question is, which do we give to Walsh?"

"If Walsh wants something in exchange for the recordings, I say we don't let on to the woman. Being in between the two of them is a risky move and she's our fail-safe."

Jase's gaze drops and his nod is nearly imperceptible.

I continue, "We don't want to get deeper into it. We just need the evidence he has on us to vanish."

"You think he'll really hand them over?" Declan asks.

"If he trusts us." I explain, "I think trust would be easier to get if we keep the information about the woman and Marcus to us. Keep it business."

"We give him a list of Marcus's men that could lead him to Marcus. In return, he gives us the recordings," Jase says as if he's testing how he feels about the deal.

"It seems like a fair trade to me," I respond and sit back in the seat, attempting to relax but every muscle in me is tight, knowing Marcus knows about Laura.

"I don't trust him," Declan pipes up.

"We don't have a choice but to trust him." Jase answers before I have to.

The sky darkens by the minute behind Jase.

"I'll give him the list," Jase decides. "I'll leave it in his mailbox at the station. We keep the intel on her and eyes on her just in case Walsh wants to fuck us over, but this way he can find Marcus."

Gripping the arms of the chair, I nod, letting go of the tension and uncertainty. It's out of my control. All I can do is hope this is enough for Walsh and that he keeps his end of the deal. And that he finds Marcus. I want him—and everything he knows—out of the picture.

Just as I'm about to stand and leave, Jase asks, "Any other updates?"

I eye him questioningly, feeling my expression show my

confusion. "On what front?" I ask him.

He cocks his brow and when I glance down at Declan, he's smirking, pulling the stack of papers in front of him into his lap. He's highlighted a few things, but most of them appear to be drawings. Locations where Marcus may be or go to often.

"Did you ask Laura about her dad?" Jase asks and coldness sweeps along my skin. Any confusion, any ease, vanishing in an instant. Dread is a prickly fucker, crawling along my skin.

"No. No updates."

"We aren't..." Declan clears his throat, his posture shifting and humor leaving at my response. "We're not trying to piss you off."

His explanation doesn't mean shit to me. "I told you—"

"Yes, she's yours," Declan says, interrupting me. "Very possessive male of you." Declan's joke doesn't help. All I can think about is what Laura would do if she knew the truth about her father. *What she'd think...*

"Just asking if everything on that front is all right?"

"Just fine," I answer Jase. Standing, I fasten a single button on my jacket.

"I'd feel better about you seeing her if it didn't turn you into a stone wall."

Jase and Declan look up at me, both waiting. I debate on telling them something, anything. A protectiveness overwhelms me when it comes to Laura. The less anyone knows, the better.

Just like Delilah, Marcus and Walsh. Just the fact that we know anything at all about them, creates a weakness that anyone can exploit. I don't want any more of that for Laura than there already is.

"Bethany asked me how you're doing last night," Jase says and exhales audibly, standing to walk to the bar on the other side of the office. "She's prying and wants information about what you're thinking in regard to her friend."

"You can tell her you don't know anything," I suggest and then hold a hand up to signal no when he offers me whiskey. Declan nods though, so Jase pulls out two glasses and they clink as he shakes his head, his lips forming a thin line.

"I did and she told me to ask."

"You sound pussywhipped."

"I'd like to make her happy, Seth. In case Walsh fucks us and I end up having to go away for a while," Jase admits harshly, his words drenched with the fear of the unknown. He takes a swig of his own drink before handing Declan his and taking a seat once again. All the while I stand and watch the emotions play on his face.

"You really like her? Is that something I could tell her?" he asks with a defeated tone.

For a moment, for some fucked-up reason, I see Derrick sitting there instead of him. I see the man I left behind. The friend who defended Laura. My partner who I couldn't look at anymore because he wanted Laura back just like I did, and he was man enough to admit it. Man enough to keep in contact with her and he had the balls to look me in the eyes and tell me.

It's been years since I've said a word to him. In this moment I want to tell him. I want to tell him I have her back.

"I've missed her and I don't plan on letting her go so easily this time."

Jase nods, again his focus drifting to nothingness behind us before he asks, "Was that so hard?"

He has no idea how much it fucking hurts to say that I missed her out loud to anyone. Telling her is brutal, telling anyone else? Agony.

"We don't know the history. But if you need to talk," Declan offers, leaving the suggestion that they're there for me implied.

A question nags in the back of my head. "Did Bethany tell you anything about me and Laura I should know?"

"Nothing apart from her thinking that Laura still loves you but she's afraid you don't love her back."

His statement hardens me. Love is a word and nothing more to Laura.

You don't leave someone if you love them.

With my jaw clenched I debate on saying just that, but it shows more about me than anything else. Parts of me they don't need to know about. My phone pings and I'm grateful for the distraction until I read the text.

My blood turns to ice and I have to read it again.

"What's wrong?" Declan asks.

"Laura just thanked me for the flowers." I'm not even cognizant that I answered him until he speaks again.

"Then why do you look like—"

I cut off the question and do my damnedest to keep my expression from showing how close to the edge of recklessness I am. "I didn't send her any flowers."

Chapter 10

Laura

I felt eyes on me the moment I got out of my car and walked into the doors of the Rockford Center. It's a weird prickling sensation that claws at me from behind.

Even now, as I pick up the tray with the last two cups of pills on it, I swear I can feel someone watching me. It's an eerie feeling. As I slowly turn, just peeking over my shoulder toward the elevators, I truly expect someone to be there.

This late at night, most of the patients are settled into their beds. Visiting hours are over. I tell myself no one is here, but I can't help but feel that I'm wrong. Call it my gut instincts.

I anticipate someone staring at me, but all I find are the simple silver doors, closed and the night hall quiet.

Letting go of a breath I didn't know I was holding, I make

my way in my favorite scrubs, a pair of white ones with deep red roses on them, to my last two patients.

They were supposed to get their pills five minutes ago, but the patient I checked on before them refused to take his. It took me a while to convince him the pills are helping, not hurting. Schizophrenia is a bitch.

That patient comes and goes as if this place is a revolving door. He never keeps up with his medication when he leaves. His symptoms get worse and he finds himself back here. Self-admitted or because his addiction and lack of employment lead him to a judge ordering him a sentence that includes a term here.

It kills.

With the thought settling deep in my gut, and the vision of that man's face in my head, I have to close my eyes just before the 3F on the door greets me. It's a calming breath that leaves me. And then another after a deep inhale.

My eyes slowly open when the prickle at my neck comes back. There's no one but me at the end of the hall. A door to my right, and across it, a door to my left. No one else is here. Aiden is in the back with the paperwork, Mel is on a smoke break. She'll be outside for at least another twenty minutes since her patients are all accounted for and sleeping. She'll do her last round, checking on their breathing, and then switch off, just like I will. We only have forty minutes left until the end of shift at 1:00 a.m.

Maybe I'm just coming down from the high I was on with Seth. The realization is sobering. That's what the odd feeling is. It's the reminder of all that happened and the fact that I was ignoring it.

The tray takes both of my hands to hold, so I have to balance it before turning the doorknob, and using my hips to bump open the door to E.J.'s room.

We weren't given her name, only initials.

Yet another thing that makes me feel uneasy. We've never had a patient whose information was guarded. We only have her medical history. Nothing else. Not a name. Not an address.

Aiden never should have accepted her in here under those conditions. With that thought resonating inside of me, I set the tray down and then look at her.

Really look at her.

Her brunette hair is matted as she lies lifeless on her side on the mattress. Her bed is made neatly, it always is, and she lies on top of it, rather than under the sheets. I know she's cold because of the goosebumps on her skin; hell, even I'm cold in this place at night.

A horrid guilt rolls through me; how could I ever think of turning someone away?

"E.J.," I say as I swallow the previous thoughts and pick up the small paper cup containing three colorful pills. And then a cup of water. I don't sit on her bed like I do with some of the other patients. I keep my distance with her, she's more receptive that way.

I sit in the chair in front of her nightstand. It hasn't moved from the last time I was in here. She doesn't like me to move it though.

It's a rare moment when I see someone in here who truly wants to die. This woman's only thirty-two, and I have no idea why since it's not in her charts and she hasn't spoken to anyone, not that she could now anyway, but she doesn't want to live another day. She has a bandage at her throat from recent surgery. The antifreeze destroyed her esophagus and she nearly died. Death's door was only a minute away from her and not for the first time either. That attempt was made in this facility and that knowledge will never leave me.

She blinks slowly and then her deep brown eyes look up at me. Rolling onto her back, she accepts the pills and then the water, downing them without thinking twice.

When she closes her eyes as I check the bandages, tears fall down her cheeks and land heavily on the bed on either side of her head.

She only sniffs once and then she swallows thickly, gripping the sheets.

"Does it hurt?" I ask her and she shakes her head. Even if she wanted to talk, her voice would be hoarse and difficult to hear. Surgery saved her life and with time, she'll be able to talk again. Not right now though, not while she's in recovery.

I wish whatever was hurting her inside would leave. I

wish it would go away. The thoughts in her head that make her desperate to die are something no one should have to deal with. I can hardly look at her without feeling her sorrow. It's palpable. Whatever happened to her, I wouldn't wish it on anyone.

"It looks like you're healing well," I comment even though I know she doesn't care. My blue gloves snap as I take them off, depositing them on the tray with the last set of pills. I never leave anything in here for E.J. I'm sure she'd think of a creative way to die with any items that are left behind.

"If you want anything at all, you know to just hit that button. I'll get you anything." Even to my own ears, I sound desperate at the last sentence. "A radio if you want music." All the rooms have televisions in the upper right corner, but she's never turned hers on.

She only shakes her head, licking the tear that had rolled its way to her lip.

"I hope you sleep well and you have the sweetest dreams," I tell her sincerely. I don't always talk to my patients like this. They're all different.

Her lips part, as if she'd say something, but she's quick to shut them. "Should I get you a pen and paper?" I ask her, but she only shakes her head again, falling back to her side and tucking her hands under her head. I leave her there, staring at the empty chair.

I'm still thinking of her when I enter the last door.

Melody's room. Which is why I nearly scream and throw my tray at the sight of a man at the end of her bed.

Thump, thump. My chest hurts from the sudden pounding.

What the hell is he doing here? It takes me more than a second to note his uniform. "Officer," I greet the man as he holds his hands out in defense.

"Nurse Roth," he says and his voice is gruff at first, but his tone and demeanor apologetic. He clears his throat, and it's only then that Melody looks up at me. She's in her young twenties and on antipsychotics. She'll more than likely be on them all her life. When she tilts her head at me as I glance between the two of them, her straight blond hair falls over her shoulder. A lock slips into her loose blouse, so loose I can see straight down and I know she's not wearing a bra. Knowing Melody, that large gray shirt is probably all she's wearing, even with this officer in the room.

It's then that I see the name tag: Walsh. *Holy fuck!*

"Melissa showed me in," the policeman explains, rising from his chair. The legs drag against the floor as he stands, pushing the chair back. With his hand held out, he introduces himself to me. "Officer Walsh."

The cold sweeps along my shoulders and down my back as I take his hand.

"You can call me Laura."

This is the first time we've met, although I know all about him from Delilah's notebook. She drew a picture of him once and I'm shocked to see how much the man in front of me looks like the sketch, but older. Years and years older.

He's good looking to say the least. Although obviously tired. The darkness under his eyes doesn't distract in the least from his pale blue eyes. I may remember pieces of what Delilah wrote about him, but I've heard other things recently. Whispers from patients who talk about Marcus. They say Walsh is a dead man for coming down here when he should have stayed in New York.

"It's nice to meet you, are you visiting?" I ask cautiously and he shakes his head as I thought he would.

"I have questions to ask Miss Trabott."

Setting the tray down on the dresser I explain to him, "I don't know that Melody is in a condition to answer any questions right now. She's not well, on heavy psychotics."

"I understand that," the officer says and eyes me, looking me up and down as if he's sizing me up. It feels like he knows exactly what I'm thinking. I hope regardless of whatever he sees, he gets the impression that I'll kick him out. I have before. Authorities can either take the patients into custody, or they can leave them alone after visiting hours. This place needs to run on a schedule and with strict procedures. Cops don't get free rein just to visit. "Melody asked me to come in. She has information about a murder."

Melody's sweet when she responds, nodding and gathering her skinny legs to sit cross-legged on the bed.

"Officer, I don't know if you're aware—"

"A murder case she's a suspect in... Laura."

All of the blood drains from my face as I stand there, stunned. Melody? Murder?

"It's not just me. He has other suspects," Melody explains and her voice drags from the drugs. She talks slowly, but with purpose and there's always a sweetness behind the words. When she's alone, she rocks and hums to herself.

"Accomplices, you mean?" Officer Walsh questions her. He's kind in the way he looks at her. As if he's not accusing her of murder.

"They were good people. Don't you agree?"

Walsh's demeanor changes. "They were, but a *priest* is dead."

"Officer," I interrupt, the cup of pills in one hand, and a cup of water in the other. "I don't want to... hinder an investigation. But it's important she take these at a certain time and if she's being questioned—"

"I waive my rights; I don't need a doctor or lawyer present." Melody gives me a soft smile, as if thanking me and I ignore her.

"With all due respect, Officer, her doctor would need to approve her mental state before anything she says would be admissible in court."

Walsh searches my gaze; it's quiet. Too quiet. The way he looks at me, like he knows something I don't... I don't like it.

"I can take them," Melody pipes up just as I part my lips

to tell him he has to come back during visiting hours. She reaches up for the cups, throwing the pills back and then does the same with her cup of water. She huffs a small humorless laugh as she crumples the little white cup in her hand. "I can't believe the priest was in there," she whispers.

Tossing the small crumpled cup into the larger paper one, she sets both down on the nightstand, staring at it when she speaks. "Why would he go there?"

Officer Walsh leans forward and the movement steals my attention. He looks at me as he asks Melody, "Did you know about the others going there? Maybe just the man who hurt you?"

"I don't know anything," she answers him in a whisper, but she can't look at him.

The rush of blood that met me when I opened the door, slows to a trickle. Melody's quiet. Her gaze is still focused on the cups on the nightstand. Or something else that's there maybe. There's nothing else present except for a clock, but maybe in her mind, something else is staring back at her.

"What happened at the farm?" I ask the officer, remembering something I read a week ago. Six men were killed in a fire at a farm off the highway, just before the state line. They hadn't identified the bodies yet.

"A fire," Officer Walsh answers and I'm quick to look back at Melody. The sweet girl who hums to herself. She came in the day I read that article, which was the day after it happened.

"Five members of a gang from upstate were locked in an old cattle farm two nights ago..." He watches Melody for her reaction before adding, "And a priest."

Her eyes close solemnly and then Melody readjusts, seeking refuge with her blanket as she covers herself up to her waist.

"The five deserved it," she speaks up and then looks back at the officer. "You know that one did, you know what he did to me," she says, pressing Walsh to agree with her. Her body sways first and then the action turns to a gentle rocking. It speeds up with every passing second of silence. "I'm not sad that they're gone."

"Did the priest deserve it?" Walsh asks her and Melody's large eyes gloss over.

"I don't know," she whispers on every rock. "I don't know anything."

"I think that's enough for tonight," I say to break the moment, moving between Walsh and Melody. The officer rises, ready to object, but I don't let him. "I don't know what's right and wrong. I don't know what she did, but she's my patient. She's not well, and she's not in the right mind to talk right now. You can always take her in for questioning."

Gathering the tray, I open the door to Melody's room and wait for Walsh to leave. He tells her to feel better before leaving. She tells him good night and the exchange is odd to me.

I don't know if he's with her or against her. If he wants her to feel like he's her friend, he's certainly accomplished that.

The door closes with a resolute click. Keeping my pace even and doing everything I can to remain professional, I walk straight ahead to the end of the hall then to the left, to the nurses' station.

Slipping the tray on top of the pile, I watch as Officer Walsh signs the check-in sheet. Signing himself out.

"I appreciate you letting her talk," he says absently, not looking at me as he does. The pen hits the paper and he stares at it, looking at all the names, I guess.

His large frame towers over the small desk in front of me and it makes him appear all the more foreboding.

The manner in which he speaks throws me off. *Letting her talk*. As if he's not grateful that he was questioning her, just that she needed to get something off her chest. That's the real reason.

"You can't get reliable information from her," I tell him although I can't look him in the eyes. There are things Delilah wrote and I know they're coloring my perception of this man. "She's not in the right mind."

"She's never in the right mind," he tells me. When he closes his eyes, he runs a hand down his face, letting his need for sleep show. "She could barely focus when she first came to me."

I don't know what to say or what to think. I don't know much about her, only what's on her chart, what she prefers to eat and the songs she must like, because she hums them constantly. I'm not her therapist or her doctor. Only her nurse.

"You've talked to her a lot?" I ask him, probing to see what he knows.

He nods once and then leans against the desk with the palms of his large hands bracing him. "She came to me for help; I tried to... but the evidence." A frustrated sigh leaves him. "I did everything I could but there wasn't enough to charge him with anything and he didn't confess. I thought we were close to getting one, but he didn't give us anything."

"I'm sorry," I say automatically and search for more. "I wish things had turned out better for both of you."

Something I say makes his gaze narrow.

"How do you think she and her friends managed to pull it off?" he asks me and then clarifies. "The five men who hurt them being burned alive in the barn. How did they do it?"

"I—I don't know," I answer him and he gauges my reaction. I add, "Maybe it wasn't them?"

"They're my only suspects. A murder of revenge. That's my working theory. Five young women and men, all of whom have never stepped out of line in their lives. One night, they conspired and committed murder. How did they do it?" he questions me again.

"I can't tell you." I'm certain surprise colors my eyes when he looks at me. I'm not a cop or an investigator. I don't know why people do the things they do. I'm shocked by weekly events here. I could only imagine what transpired that led to the fire that night.

"Someone helped them," he concludes.

"Who would help them? The priest?" I take a guess, still confused and not completely on board with Walsh's working theory.

"I don't think so. I don't understand how Father John plays into all this." I can see the wheels turning in Walsh's head, trying to piece together what happened.

"If it wasn't the priest who helped them... then who?"

"Someone they see as a vigilante. That's my theory."

"A vigilante?" The longer I stand here talking to him, the more and more I feel insane. Or maybe he's the one who's lost it. My mind whirls with all the secrets I know and it makes it more difficult to pretend I don't know what he's getting at. He called Marcus a vigilante. Delilah wrote about it.

"Someone who wanted the men dead for a different reason. Someone who would benefit from the event occurring and make himself look like a hero in the process."

"Who would want them dead?" I play along, pretending I don't know what he's implying.

"You know who."

"I don't understand. I'm afraid you have me at a loss," I lie.

"Marcus. I'm sure you've heard of him. Everyone in this town has," he comments and I feel my cheeks burn. For a moment, I doubt that I've held the secret of taking Delilah's notebooks close enough. I question if he knows. Or is it just that he assumes everyone knows about Marcus? The way he looks at me, though... It feels like he knows I know all about him and all about Marcus.

"A girl is hurt, and not well. This man seeks her out, knowing he can get her to do unspeakable things in order to feel better. In order to feel like she got the justice she should have gotten from the legal system."

I don't want to know about any of this. I'm her caretaker and that's the only reason I intervened. The words are there, ready to be spoken. Instead I find myself thinking and pray I swallow the thought quickly enough that the officer doesn't see it written on my face. *Is that what happened with Delilah?*

I'm drained as I get to my loft and sag against the door. There's not an ounce of me left to keep me upright. My keys jangle as I toss them on the counter.

I'm torn when it comes to Officer Walsh. What I read about him and what I saw tonight are at odds, painting contrasting mind pictures. I don't know what to think about the man, but I can't get what he said out of my head.

I find myself slipping into old habits, inserting myself between the business of powerful men with unjust causes just as easily as I sulk to my living room to gaze at the bouquet.

Some nights I'm numb from work. It's a brutal reality

to be submerged in. That's why I told Seth I want to stay at my place after long shifts. He agreed. Nearly everything I suggested, he agreed with this morning. Technically, yesterday morning.

I sag into my sofa and then kick off my sneakers, one by one without untying them. Tonight, this exhaustion isn't from work. It's because I'm questioning my own ability to think straight.

How did I get to this point in my life where I constantly question my sanity and my judgment? When did it get this bad?

A knock at the door sounds, as if answering the question. The large black hands on the clock on the wall read 1:47. I'm hesitant to rise, but almost certain it's Seth.

There's no one else who should be here. For a moment, I question if I should get a knife. I don't have a gun and as the doorknob rattles I curse myself for that.

"Laura," Seth calls out before the door is cracked open and I let out a strangled breath. *Thank fuck.*

"Way to give me a fucking heart attack," I reprimand him although I don't have the energy to speak loud enough for him to hear me.

I'm still inwardly calming myself when Seth comes into view, closing the door behind him.

"I made myself a key," he comments, holding up the shiny silver piece in his hand and then letting it fall, clanging with the other keys on the ring. It takes me a minute to respond.

I'm too caught up in how he's dressed. There's no suit today, only faded jeans and a black t-shirt. Simple and yet everything I remember. Running his hand over the back of his head, he ruffles his hair before tossing the keys down on the counter... right next to mine.

The memories come back. Memories of how we used to do just that and it never felt wrong or off or confusing. Not like it does now.

"Of course you made yourself a key... I'd ask how, but..." I leave the thought unfinished and lean back into the sofa, gathering the throw blanket to pull over myself.

"You look good," I tell him offhandedly. Seth looks down at himself and then back at me. I cut him off before he can say a damn word. "I look like hell because that's how I feel."

"Long day?" he asks and stalks into the living room. Stalking is exactly how he goes about it too. Careful steps as he eyes my loft.

"Yeah," I answer him and then watch him. "Like what you see?" I ask and my tone hints at how pissed off I am. It's late, I'm tired, and he's come here unannounced.

"Twentieth floor loft with floor-to-ceiling windows that overlook the park," Seth says and glances outside, but it's so dark that you can't really see a damn thing. He has to pull back the thick curtains and stare for a second and then another until he concludes the same thing.

As he takes a casual seat in the dusty rose velvet chair

across from me, I tell him, "Never thought of myself as a city girl but when I moved here... I wanted a change."

I mindlessly pick at the throw blanket, as if there are little fuzzes to be plucked but there aren't.

"Dyed your hair, got your dream job and an upscale place," Seth speaks and looks anywhere but at me.

"Hey, a girl who changes her hair is a girl who's changing her life." Why does it hurt so much to say a simple quote? Is it the unspoken judgment Seth reeks of? Or is it the shame that I did just that: I ran away and changed my life.

"You're still the same girl," Seth comments and leans forward in the small chair. With his elbows on his knees he asks me, "You like it here?"

"Yeah," I answer him honestly. "It's small, but I like it a lot."

He only nods, leaning back in the chair and I have to let out a long yawn. Seth looks so out of place in here. My décor is feminine and chic. His rough edges and masculinity stand out in this room. They'd stand out anywhere though.

He's busy staring at the flowers and that's when I remember he didn't answer my text. "Hey, the number you messaged me with the other day... that's yours, right?" I ask him and he nods once. "I um... thank you for the flowers."

"I got your text," he answers and that hard lump in my chest grows. He stands from the chair and walks past me to the kitchen. I don't bother to look and I'm not surprised when I hear the sound of the fridge opening.

"Make yourself at home." My comment is complete with a full-on eye roll and then I lay my head back, resting my eyes.

"You want a drink, Babygirl?" Seth asks and I tell him no.

"If I have one, I'll pass out," I say.

When he comes back empty-handed I tell him he's welcome to whatever he wants and that I was just joking, but he shakes his head, slipping his hands into his jeans.

"If I'd known you were coming, I'd have gotten you IPA." I hint at the reason I'm a little miffed.

"See," he says as he gives me a weak smile, "same girl."

The way he looks at me melts something inside that hurts. Something that's not meant to burn. "Not all the same," I murmur, pulling my legs into my chest. I've fallen asleep here too many times to count. Work's draining and the long shifts are hard on me some days.

Days like today.

"They remind me of the flowers I got you," he says as he steps slowly toward them and pauses to observe the bouquet.

"They are them." I can practically hear the simper that lingers on my lips in my voice when I tell Seth, "I'd never forget.

"Cami said it was a sign that you'd gotten both my favorite flowers and hers. She used to joke that the buttercups were her favorite and the flowers were really meant for her as a thank you for..." I trail off as I almost tell him how she pushed me to kiss him. Cami urged me to go after what I wanted and to stop thinking. Seth didn't make the moves first. He always let me do it. Times have changed.

"Buttercups?"

"The ranunculus. These ones," I say and I have to lean forward to reach. I don't like the way he looks down at me when I look up at him. He's uncertain; I can see it so clearly.

The realization makes me withdraw, pulling the throw blanket tighter around me before tossing it off altogether. I'm falling into old habits, when I shouldn't. Everything is different now.

"I have to wash my face and get ready for bed," I tell him with a sigh as I stand up. "I had a twelve-hour shift and another tomorrow."

There's only so much a person can take. I aim to walk around him, but he stops me, cupping my elbow in his hand and then pulling me into his chest. *Have I ever given into his warmth as easily as I do now?* Sagging into his chest without hesitation. Closing my eyes and breathing him in. My arms wrap around him and I hold him lightly as he pets my hair and then plants a kiss on my temple.

"I'm tired," I whisper. "And I don't know what we are." Insecurity rises and with the last statement my eyes open. "What are we doing?" I ask him.

With sleep pulling me under, it's hard to remember why I gave myself to him last night.

"We're feeling better," he reminds me.

It's difficult to imagine that this is better. With all the

doubt surrounding me.

"Do you forgive me for leaving you?" The moment the question is spoken, I wish I could take it back. Seth's warm embrace turns stiff and it takes a long moment before he answers, "Don't asks questions you don't want the answers to."

A sad smile plays along my lips. It turns sadder when he goes about petting my hair again and the arm he has around my waist holds me closer to him.

Maybe one day. I don't believe the thought enough to speak it.

Peeking up from his hold, I get a good look at the tattoo on his bicep. The thin lines are clean but so close to one another, I can only imagine the ink will bleed together and all it will be is a solid black ring.

"You got more," I comment and run my finger along them.

"More years to remember," he tells me solemnly.

"Didn't you skip a year?" I say but my memory is so foggy.

He only looks down at me questioningly. His eyes are tired and he needs to shave. "Your stubble's turning into a beard."

He doesn't say anything, again he only watches me as I leave his embrace, making my way to the bathroom. It's hot and cold with him and I don't know what to think.

"Is there anyone else?" he finally asks the moment I turn to go to the bathroom and get on with bed, with or without him.

"Anyone else?" The confusion settles into a crease in my forehead.

"Are you seeing anyone else?"

"No." I huff out the response. "I haven't seen anyone in… over a month now."

"Good. When I said you're mine, I meant it." His tone is hard and unforgiving, like I've done something wrong.

"Why do you want me?" I breathe out with exasperation.

"To have you when I want." Seth's answer is bullshit and selfish.

So I hurt him back. "That's the only reason you ever kept me, isn't it?"

"Only reason you ever stayed, isn't it?" My response may have been a slap to the face. His is a bullet to my heart.

With my back to him, I sulk to the bathroom, turning on the faucet to run as hot as it can. With a hand on either side of the sink, I stare at the clear water swirling down the drain, waiting for the steam to come.

Seth isn't quiet when he comes up behind me, and I meet his gaze in the mirror.

"I mean it," Seth says again like it's a warning.

"Mean what?" I say and whip around, pissed off.

"You're mine."

"Seth… I am very much aware of that." It's all I can say. I won't deny it.

"Good." He gives the one-word response before grabbing my thighs and pulling me into his arms. His touch is fire, possessive and full of need.

It shocks me. Even as my back hits the tiled wall of the bathroom and his lips crash against mine. The wind is knocked out of me from the sudden wave of desire.

His fingers dig into my flesh as my legs wrap around his hips. His hard touch softens as he nips my bottom lip and pulls back, breathless.

With his body pressed against me and my hands on his muscular chest, I stare into his eyes wanting to know what the hell has gotten into him.

Before I can speak, he nudges his nose against mine and my eyes close from the tender touch. He kisses me once, short and soft.

Then he kisses me again and this time he deepens it. The water's still running, but I couldn't care less. I moan into his mouth and let him love me the way he knows how.

He nips my bottom lip, my breasts pressing flat against his chest as he leans forward, pinning me where I am.

Instantly, I'm hot and I feel suffocated. I crane my neck, to breathe cooler air, and he takes that as a sign to rake his teeth down my neck. The hint of pain as he drags his teeth and then bites down on my shoulder only ignites pleasure deep down in my belly and then lower.

"Seth," I moan.

"I fucking love it when you say my name," he groans in the crook of my neck before picking me up, one arm keeping me pinned to him.

He turns off the water, turns off the light. He doesn't ask at all if I was done. I hadn't even begun but none of it matters.

With the lights still off in my bedroom, he lays me down, never separating his body from mine and continues his slow, deliberate nips and kisses down my body. He peels my clothes down as he goes. When he gets to my waist, I have to prop myself up to take off my shirt. With my arms above my head, the shirt covering my face for just a moment, Seth unhooks my bra and viciously sucks my nipple. Gasping, I arch my back, and nearly buck him away from me because of the sudden onslaught of pleasure. He's everywhere at once, his hands, his lips, his hard body pinning me down, feeling my curves, worshiping every inch of me.

He only breaks long enough to remove his own shirt and then his pants after he's removed mine.

With both of us naked and panting he braces himself over me, in the perfect position to have me. I can't help but to reach up and kiss him, again and again, on his jaw, his lips, down to his neck. My touch isn't as rough and primal as his, but it's just as needy.

"Touch yourself," Seth says, pulling back when I kiss him again. My lips brush against his, the electricity vibrating through my body. It takes me a moment, my head spinning with desire to realize what he said.

"What?"

"You heard me," he commands, "touch yourself the way

you did when you thought about me."

Thump. My heart pounds from the tone of his voice.

Unconsciously my left leg wraps around his thigh, wanting to urge him on, to have him lose control with me.

"I want you," I whisper, practically begging him.

"Touch yourself first, Babygirl." The depths of his eyes reflect only lust and that gives me hope in the uncertainty of what he's doing. "I want you to know the difference," he says, his voice deep and jagged with his own need that he's resisting. "I need you to feel what you can do all by yourself and then feel what I give you."

I crash my lips against his frantically and before he can pull away, my right hand moves to my clit. My nipples are pebbled against his chest and every small movement feels like heaven against them.

A small protest of a moan slips by me when Seth sits up on his knees, watching me in the dark bedroom as I touch myself beneath him. My head falls to the side as I circle my clit, but Seth's quick to put an end to that.

With his hand on my throat, he forces me to look up. "I want to see you," he whispers roughly with his other hand wrapped around his cock and I cum, just like that. I could see him stroking himself as I do the same to myself and the very thought of him losing himself on me was my undoing.

"So easy," he teases me in a murmur, leaning down to kiss me as the waves of my orgasm rock through me, heating my skin, paralyzing my senses in overwhelming pleasure.

Before the pleasure has waned, Seth grips my hips and flips me onto my belly in a swift movement that causes me to yelp in surprise. Lying flat on my belly, he teases my entrance, his thick head probing and playing.

"So easy, so wet. Tell me it's just for me."

With my eyes closed his command envelops me. Of course it's just for him. It's always been him.

"Just for you. It's all just for you." I barely get the words out, still struggling to breathe. In a forceful stroke, Seth enters me, brutally and with a blinding pleasure that has me screaming his name. My nails dig into the sheets and a cold sweat layers every inch of my skin. He waits a moment, his forearm brushing my shoulder until his front is against my back. Simply hovering over me, touching me although his weight doesn't push me down.

"You were made for me," he whispers at the shell of my ear, slipping his hand between my hip and the bed, not stopping until his fingers brush my clit. "This is how you did it?" he questions.

"Yes," I answer quickly and honestly.

He circles my clit and I bury my face into the sheets, moaning low in my throat from the sweet, decadent pull in my core. Bringing me closer to the edge once again. Just as a sheen of heat lifts from my body, as the coiled pleasure threatens to burst, Seth thrusts his hips, never relenting in the attention he pays to my swollen and sensitive nub. And again, and again. Picking up his pace and steadily fucking me deep and raw and possessively.

I have to bite down on the sheets. I try to move away from him; it's all too much. At the same time, I want more, I want him deeper, I want to feel him pulsing inside of me.

"Seth." The only word I can say is his name. Even the friction between my breasts and the sheets is igniting as he ruthlessly fucks me from behind.

He made his point with the first thrust. He made his point without even touching me. I know I can never have what he gives me with anyone else, let alone my own touch. He doesn't stop though, not until my voice is hoarse and raw, my body and lips tingling with a heated sensation that feels like it will last forever.

Chapter 11

Seth

Parked in the lot across from the Rockford Center, the police station is about a mile down the road and easily monitored. From here, in the driver side of my car with the window rolled down, the cop cars come and go, seemingly insignificant at a distance. I remember a time when I'd get anxious from just the thought of one.

Time changes a lot of things.

An old man in blue jeans and a thin dark gray hoodie mows the circular patch of grass out front of the large cement building directly in front of me.

Other than the small garden of roses on either side of the sidewalk that divides the grass, there's no color at all. The upper half of the three-story building is painted gray. The lower half is the same shade as cement.

Men and women go in and out of the Rockford Center, but the police station is far busier. There's only been a handful of nurses, out on smoke breaks, the mailman and now the gardener taking up residence out here. Even the parking lot is barren. Employees park around back and that leaves only myself and one other parked car with no one occupying it in this lot.

It's an odd choice to plant roses in a place like this.

It reminds me of a book we had to read in school, *I Never Promised You a Rose Garden*. It was about some girl in a place like this. I didn't read it, Laura did though. She cried at the end. I wonder if she likes the roses out front, or if they make her want to cry like the book did.

The smell of freshly cut grass hits me as the breeze drifts into the car. Picking up the paper bag next to me, I realize the sandwich inside it isn't quite hot anymore. It's still warm though.

I must've been sitting out here for longer than I realized. At least the coffee is still hot. I picked up everything from the corner diner by the bar; they have the best coffee in town. It's something sweet, caramel drizzle, or some shit like that, for Laura.

She may have eaten lunch already. I don't know. My phone's been in my hand, the bag on the passenger seat, and all the while, I've just been sitting here, watching, not going in.

The flowers have fucked with my head more than they should. They're just too much like the ones I gave her. It's unsettling. It feels like a sign or something. A signal that what we're doing is wrong. That it's not supposed to be this way.

I always knew I'd see Laura again, talk to her. Sometimes my thoughts would be only of a moment. One moment where we recognized each other and maybe even kissed, but never more than that.

A girl at the bar one night talked about star-crossed lovers and ever since she rattled on about it, I wondered if that's what we were meant to be. Because every time I'm around her, it hurts and I know it hurts her too.

It's like falling down a spiral where nothing else matters; I can't even see anything but her when she's in front of me. But I know I'm falling. Some falls you don't recover from.

Last night, sleep evaded me, the image of the flowers and reckless thoughts haunting me every time I closed my eyes.

My phone pings and I'm grateful to be ripped from my thoughts. The message I get isn't what I want to see though. Cursing under my breath, I don't respond.

Declan's got nothing.

The box the flowers came in was in the trash in her kitchen. I searched for it the second she passed out last night. It didn't have any identifying information. No note, no nothing. Declan can't find a record of any flowers ordered online to be delivered to Laura's address either.

It doesn't sit right with me.

If she wants to believe they came from me though, I'll let her believe it.

It's something more though, something unsettling deep in my bones. It feels like a warning. Like her leaving me is going to happen all over again. I barely survived the last time. She's the same, better even. But me? I'm a fucking shell of the man I was when I was with her.

Declan messages again and I have to respond to his text which reads: *Did he get the list?*

Looking past the center and to the police station, as if I can see Walsh opening the note I dropped in his box outside his office, I text Declan back: *Yeah. I left it at his office. A list of all six names with the note, they'll lead you to the man you're looking for.*

Declan sends a series of texts and I read them one by one. Little things he's wondering about from the copies of the diaries he has. He wants me to read them to get an idea of what I think about his conclusions. It's years of scattered thoughts from a tormented woman and right now, that's the last thing I want to do.

"Seth?" Laura says my name like it's a question.

"Shit," I hiss and get over the jolt that pinned me to the back of my seat. My back teeth grind and I have to unclench the paper bag to put it down. "You like scaring the shit out of me, don't you?"

My comment comes as I shake off the unease of being startled without her knowing. Her smile never falters. With her hair pulled high into a bun on the top of her head and a pair of scrubs with a print of coffee cups and hearts, she looks like she doesn't belong here. It's too much sweetness for a place that's made of stone.

"I thought it was you sitting out here." She rocks on her heels before lowering herself to the open window, folding her arms over it and getting closer to me. "I needed some fresh air... didn't expect to see you."

It strikes me for a moment how easy she makes it seem. Like there was no hesitation, no reason she shouldn't come to me.

My gaze darts to her lips as she licks them and the wind rushes, making her shiver.

"I was just thinking of you and brought you some coffee."

"As an apology for keeping me up all night?" she jokes and then hums, "Smells good."

Grabbing the bag and the coffee, I hold them in my lap. "Kiss first."

As the smile grows on her face, so does something warm inside of me. Something that covers the nagging feeling that everything's wrong. It comes with that first step down the spiral staircase. Blindly moving. Just like she does when she lets me hold her chin between my thumb and forefinger and steal a kiss from her. And then another.

There's always another when it comes to her.

Chapter 12

Laura

"God I wish Bethany were here."

"Anything I can help you with?" Aiden asks me and it's only then that I realize I spoke the thought out loud.

"Oh, no. No, just... nothing." I force a smile to my face and tap the pen in my hand on the chart. "All good," I tell him when he doesn't look away.

He keeps looking a moment longer, even after I turn my attention back to Melody's sheet.

My coffee's lukewarm now, but it hits the spot as I take a nice long sip and then look at the clock. One more hour until things wind down.

"She'll be here tomorrow." Aiden's comment reminds me that he's still standing by the nurses' station. "I have to say, I missed her."

"This *place* missed her," I say then add, "I'm glad she'll be back to pick up some of these rounds."

Aiden's chuckle isn't forced and it reminds me that he's a nice guy. I haven't been able to think of him the same since E.J. was admitted. It's hard not to think of it as a political decision. The check was big enough, so he let the rules slide for her.

Whoever has her here, with her information hidden, they want her alive and taken care of. I guess that's all that matters.

I watch him leave, waving at Mel who's counting pills that go into each of the little cups behind the half wall with a windowpane for the upper half.

Just as I'm returning the clipboard, I get that nagging prick that someone's watching me on the back of my neck and instead of being quiet about it, I whip around quickly, fear gripping my heart in a cold vise that chills my body.

The back of a black hoodie and dark jeans disappears behind the corner to the hall where my patients are.

I don't like it. Not the look of him or the feeling that resonates in my gut. Grabbing the sign-in sheet for a half second, I don't see a new name. No one signed in recently and I know every name on this list. Every single one. His name isn't here and it damn well should be.

My strides are purposeful as I round the corner.

"Excuse me," I call out, eager to get to the man as he nears the very end of the hall. He stops between the doors that lead to either Melody or E.J.

When he turns around, he tilts his head questioningly and a thin scar on his chin shines from the fluorescent lights above us.

"Do you mind signing in, please?" I ask him cordially, through an innate dread that creeps along every inch of my skin. He's handsome, although rough around the edges. Something about him... my soul doesn't like him.

"Yeah, yeah," the guy says as he smiles at me, and it's a charming smile, with perfect teeth. It makes him look younger too, but it doesn't reach his eyes. He scratches his chin, at the scar, maybe in an attempt to hide it. "This way?" he questions me, urging me to walk with him and I don't want to. The need to check on both the patients beyond those doors rides me harder than anything else in this moment. He was headed to one of them.

It's then that I realize it's quiet, there's no one else here. No patients on their way to the game room or the library. No visitors other than this man in the lone hall and every door down this way is closed.

"Yes. Let me show you," I speak politely, hiding everything I'm feeling and brushing aside my nerves. I feel paranoid. Shaking my head, I breathe out in exasperation.

"Something I said?" the visitor asks. His blondish hair is long enough that it tousles as he walks next to me.

"No, sorry. Just something I was thinking about before

I saw you." I direct him to the clipboard, picking up the pen and holding it out to him. He takes it, but not quickly enough. His slender fingers linger. Standing this close to him, I note that he's taller than me. He doesn't carry a lot of weight to him, but he's lean and toned.

The cords in his throat tense when he says, "Thank you."

Shoving my hands into my pockets, I only nod.

"Who are you here for?" I ask him when I see he's only filled out his name. Jacob something. I can't quite read his last name from this angle.

"Just checking on a friend is all," he says softly, with a hint of an accent although I can't place it. Southern, maybe?

I'm stern but still polite, still kind even, when I explain, "You have to write—"

"Laura." I'm cut off by a familiar voice.

Officer Walsh nods a greeting at Jacob, and then apologizes for interrupting. After looking at the silver watch, which looks expensive and doesn't match the read I got on Jacob, the visitor who never said who he was visiting, tells Officer Walsh it's all right and he has to get back to work anyway.

I watch the man go, not listening to a damn word coming from Officer Walsh.

"Do you know him?" I ask the man to my left, a police officer who should have the kind of sense about a person that I've learned to have.

He blinks at me once, his thick lashes covering those pale

blue eyes for a moment before his brow raises and he catches sight of the black hoodie just as the elevator doors close.

"Should I?" Officer Walsh asks me.

I debate on telling him the thoughts that are racing through my mind. "Did he do something?" Officer Walsh asks, widening his stance to face me and moving his head lower so he cuts off my view of the elevator doors.

In this moment, Walsh looks trustworthy, *feels* trustworthy. "Tell me now, Laura. I can go get him. Just tell me."

Although it's a command, he speaks so softly, with such empathy, I almost tell him how I don't have a good feeling about that guy.

But he's a cop for fuck's sake and feelings aren't evidence of shit.

I shrug and say, "Just rubbed me the wrong way for some reason."

"Don't take gut instincts for granted," Walsh advises and then he seems to remember he has to sign in. He does, marking Melody down as well. "Maybe it's good I got here when I did."

A chill flows over my shoulders, as if agreeing with him.

"Maybe," I agree. Peeking over my shoulder, I watch Mel separate more cups on a new tray.

"You're here for more questions?" I ask him, changing the subject.

"I thought you would prefer it if I came during visitor hours."

I don't hesitate to tell him, "You thought right." He

gives me a tight smile and nods, nearly walking away but then he stops to tell me, "You're protective of them. That's a good thing."

I search his eyes, wrinkled at the edges from his genuine smile and then ask, "Why not bring her in if you think she did it?"

He pauses, looking down at the linoleum floor before slipping his hands into the pockets of his dark blue uniform pants. "She was in a support group before this. She needed to be."

"She needs more than a support group," I urge him. I want to tell him that she's so much better after the therapy sessions. And after a week of regular medication, she's more active, carrying on more conversations than normal. "She's doing well here."

"I'm not suggesting that she's not." He runs his hand over his chin and tells me, "Sometimes... people need justice. And it's hard to define what that is. Five men died that night and in my opinion, they should have been dead long before it for the things they'd done and gotten away with. My job is to protect and serve. It's not so different from yours when you think about it."

"So you don't want to take her in even though you think she did it... because you're okay that she did it."

"I didn't say that," he replies and shakes his head. "I just need to be sure that what I'm doing will help her."

"Do you think she really did it? You still have the theory

that Marcus helped her and the others get revenge." Saying Marcus's name to Walsh seems wrong and makes me uneasy but he doesn't react, he doesn't even look away from the sign-in sheet. Not until he speaks again.

"I think she knew and what I found today... I think she knew about the priest being there and I want to know why."

His admission startles me. "There was only one name on the list of confessors before the priest left. Witnesses verify he left the church a quarter after seven. It was Melody's name—she was the last one to see him before he burned to death with the rest of them."

"And still... you aren't going to bring her in?"

"She has motive for one of the murders. We have circumstantial evidence now for the priest. That's all I've got."

I nod, understanding. "If she confesses here though... would it count?"

A sad smile graces his lips. "Count?" He rocks on his heels and looks up at the ceiling before swallowing tightly. "I don't want her," he admits to me in almost a whisper. His pale blue eyes seek mine out, begging me to understand.

"You want Marcus," I surmise.

"That's all I want. If she can give me something on him..."

"What about the others? Her friends from the support group. The ones you think came up with all this? Why don't you ask them?"

"I have. No one mentioned Marcus or admitted to

anything. I know Melody's case. I'd spoken to her when she came to me a couple of months ago. I think that's the only reason she's opened up. She's the only one who's given me anything. She's the one with remorse."

I could point out that she's also drugged and not in her right mind, but I bite down on that thought in favor of something else. "Have you brought them in? The others to question them?"

"I don't want to. The thing is, there isn't an ounce of me that thinks they'll do something like this again. I also don't believe they would have done it at all had Marcus not urged them to do it. Given them the solution and laid out the plan."

"Do you know that's what happened for sure?" I ask him. "Sometimes people do things… you don't expect."

"Trust me, I've seen my share. It's my gut feeling. Marcus will never stop. Since I've shown up, the death rate has only increased. He's keeping me busy."

I struggle, knowing more about Officer Walsh and Marcus than he realizes. I feel like a crook and a liar.

"I have questions for Miss Melody." Walsh plasters a thin, short-lived smile on his face.

"Officer," I say and stop him, feeling compelled to say something, "if there's anything I can do to help, please let me know."

A genuine smile replaces the forced one. "I appreciate that."

Chapter 13

Seth

Watching a clock is a shit way to eat up time. But then again, so is staring at a phone screen, wishing you were reading a different message.

I called Derrick about Fletcher a few days ago and asked if there was any talk of him or his crew recently. I killed Fletcher before he could kill me. It's that simple. Along with him, I took out all of his men who had any authority. I let them scatter. His name shouldn't be breathed by anyone of relevance.

Derrick said he'd look into it.

Today he sent me a response. It was detailed and thorough, with the names and addresses of five men who still hang together and were a part of Fletcher's crew.

That's all I've got. That was the last message he sent.

It was an hour ago that the text came through. And fifty minutes since I responded *thanks*.

It's the first time I've talked to him in years. This is all that's between us now. Business. The small clock on the mantel ticks and I pick up my beer, setting down one of the folders on the coffee table, taking a large swig before sending Derrick another message.

How are things?

My eyes burn from reading the handwritten print for hours. It's all I've been doing: putting together the puzzle pieces written in the journals. The problem is Delilah contradicts herself. The locations are something we can work with, but the other things she's written... I don't know that I trust them. She's not a reliable source and it's frustrating and time consuming. If it leads to Marcus though, it'll all be worth it.

I try to remember the last real conversation I had with Derrick. It was about Laura, I know that. He wanted me to come back, he said he wanted me *whole*. All he ever talked about was Laura. He hung Cami's death over my head, reminding me that he'd never be all right again, but I could still chase after what I lost. Laura was still out there.

Damn, that has to be three years ago.

Are you with her? Derrick asks me in the text and my eyes narrow, my head tilts. There's no reason he should know that I am. I looked through her messages, searching for someone who could have sent her flowers; they haven't spoken in years.

She told the truth when she said she hadn't spoken to him a long damn time.

Why do you ask? I write him back.

Fuck off with that. I'm still your right-hand man.

I huff a humorless laugh and it comes with a slight smirk. Leaning back on the sofa, I read the message, settling the beer bottle to rest on my thigh. Those were good times. When he was my right hand and Laura was my girl.

She'll be here in an hour when she gets off work, I text and then add, *She's a nurse now.* It's not until I send it that I realize he already knows. She'd already finished school four years ago so when they were talking, I'm sure she told him.

I know, he confirms. *She still loves you too.*

It's not like that, I text him and feel a deep ache settle in my chest. It'll never be what it was.

I down the beer and get up to retrieve another, leaving the phone where it is. It pings the moment I get to the fridge.

Opening the beer, taking a sip, I make my way back and read the message only to feel that anxiousness I was drinking down, creeping back up.

There's something you should know. They found a body at the warehouse. Does Laura know about her dad?

No. Setting the beer down, I feel the cold prick along my skin. *No one needs to look into that.* Years have gone by without her father being a blip on my radar. I don't like him being brought up.

They don't need to, but the evidence is there. She may find out either way.

I mutter *fuck* and close my eyes. Dread is a bitter taste in my mouth. *She can't know*, I text him back.

You've got her now. Just don't let her go. No matter what comes out.

Derrick's texts come hurriedly, one after the other.

I remind him, *I asked how you were*, wanting to get off this subject. I can't handle this right now. Not when I don't know if there's even a reason to be concerned. My stomach churns, knowing Laura's father is on Marcus's radar though. Maybe the evidence is already out and he found it before putting the pieces together.

There's a lot of shit that's changed since you left, but overall, things are good.

I text him the obvious question to move things away from business: *You got a girl?*

A minute passes before he answers, *Not yet. I have to go, but I'll keep you updated with anything going on at the warehouse.*

Thanks.

With that, I'm left with just my beer, too many questions I don't have answers to, and the time ticking down.

Derrick used to ask me if I was punishing myself or Laura. The memory of the last conversation we had comes back full force. I can hear his voice in my head, asking me that question like he was some kind of fucking therapist.

Maybe it was a punishment to be so close to her, but not have her. Although, I couldn't have known she wouldn't come to me. For weeks, I thought she'd learn I was here, that I was close to her, and she'd come to me. When her name came up on the alert and I knew she was searching my name online, it put an end to that speculation.

The alarm beeps and a moment later the headlights from Laura's sedan shine through the front window. We spent last night at her place, tonight we stay here. I know she's had a long shift, but my place is closer to the center, so it was easy enough to get her to agree.

I don't know what we are. I don't know why my head's so fucked. But I know she's mine. She'll stay here until I tell her otherwise.

Laura comes into the house the same way I came into her place last night, saying my name as she pushes open the door with a key in her hand.

"You found it," I say as I smirk at her. Even after a twelve-hour shift in baggy scrubs, she's breathtaking.

"The key in my sandwich bag? Yes, yes I did."

"It was unlocked, you know?" I tease her.

"Maybe I wanted to make sure it was to your front door. Since, you know, it just happened to be in the bag with no note." She shrugs as she adds, "It could have been anyone's key."

"It's yours."

Closing and then locking the door behind her, she cradles an overnight bag in the crook of her arm along with her purse. It's not a large bag and I'm sure she only packed for one night. I'll have to fix that. She needs everything here and a place for what she needs in the cabinets and dressers. I'll correct that issue tomorrow. Dropping her keys next to mine on the kitchen counter, she leaves her bag there too and rubs her eyes, sagging into the seat next to me.

I hold up the beer, offering it to her but she shakes her head and then rests her forehead on my shoulder, sleep weighing her down. "You don't drink after work. Now that is different."

She smiles in the crook of my neck and her shoulders shake slightly with a small feminine snicker.

Glancing up at me, she gives me a smile and then rolls to the side, giving me space. She lets out an exhausted yawn and tells me she's just tired.

"Bethany said I should take up a red wine nightcap to help me sleep."

"I'll grab a couple of bottles."

"Mmm," she half responds with her eyes closed. Eyeing her plump lips with a loose tendril of hair in her face has me hard in a split second.

"You're not allowed to sleep just yet," I tell her and those long lashes sweep up so she can look at me.

"I should probably tell you something first," she says and

the sweetness and playful demeanor fall from her expression until all I see is my tired girl.

Setting down the beer and leaning forward, I pray it's not about someone calling from California with news on her father. I'm aware of how I tell her to tell me, relaxed and easy. I'm aware of how I'm breathing calmly, like I'm not worried at all.

"Walsh came by the center." Relief hits first, then pride when Laura looks down at her hands, watching her fingers wring around one another as she tells me, "Today and yesterday."

She feels guilty for not telling me. I like the look of submission on her.

"Did he talk to you?" I ask her, expecting to hear that he didn't. Why would he? He doesn't know she's with me. He doesn't know shit about her. Or about the diaries.

"He did. About a murder and one of my patients." She readjusts and then looks at my beer where I left it. "Maybe I should have a drink," she comments.

"I'll get you one; you keep talking," I tell her and stand up, moving away from her field of vision to listen.

"The fire that happened down at the farm." She speaks louder so I can hear as I open cabinets, pretending to look for a stray bottle of wine. Crouched down and staring at rows of clear and amber liquor bottles, I listen. "He thinks she has motive and it has something to do with Marcus helping her get revenge."

"The fire at the farm?" I question her, as I stand up and move to the fridge. "No wine, Babygirl," I add with a smile, easing her as much as I can.

"A beer?" she asks and even pouts. She can't know how I want to kill Walsh for talking to her. She can't know half the shit that's going on. She wouldn't want to anyway. If she knew, she wouldn't stay.

"The thing is," she keeps talking as I twist the top off and toss it in the garbage. She only stops talking to thank me when I retake my seat next to her. "He keeps bringing up Marcus. He's talking to me as if he knows that I know."

My hackles rise, the tiny hairs on my arms standing on edge.

"Whether he knows about the diaries or he thinks I've heard things and whispers in the center... I don't know."

"What did you tell him?"

"I played dumb. I told him if he needs anything from me, to let me know."

Her nervousness and insecurity are something I've never liked. I'm here and as long as I'm here, she shouldn't feel like that. I'll fix it. I'll find out everything and fix it.

"A cop came in questioning a murder, that's... nerve wracking," I answer her, taking a long drag of my beer after handing Laura hers. She doesn't move to drink yet; even though I'm staring at the fireplace, I know she's staring at me. "To add on to it, you have secrets. You know about him and his motives. That's what's gotten to you," I say as I finally look at her and rest my hand on her thigh.

I have to give her a small smirk when my gentle touch, the back and forth of my thumb, gives her shivers. A deep chuckle vibrates up my chest. "So easy," I tease her.

She finally smiles, a cute little smile that she tries to catch between her teeth. The soft pink of a blush rises to her cheeks and she asks me, "You really think that's all this is?"

"You don't like secrets and you're shit at keeping them," I tell her. "You're doing good." Patting her thigh and then giving a gentle squeeze, I tell her, "Don't worry about Marcus or Walsh. They don't know anything and it's all in that pretty little head of yours."

"You sure?" Even though she questions me, her body language relaxes. Everything about her believes me. Which is shit, because I'm lying to her. Marcus knows something. Walsh doesn't though.

I give her a smile, followed by a peck of a kiss that leaves her with her eyes closed and a simper on her lips. "I'm sure, Babygirl. You're just stressed, but you handled it well."

"It's just a lot and it feels like—"

I cut her off to say, "Because it is a lot. You're carrying a heavy burden on your shoulders every day. When someone makes you question yourself, it feels a lot worse, knowing everything else that could fall." Cupping her chin in my hand, I kiss her again. I swear every time we kiss she melts a little more. She doesn't worry, she doesn't buy into the voices in her head telling her she's not enough and she's in too deep. I should kiss her every moment of every day.

"So... what should I do?" she asks me.

"You already handled it. Nothing else to do but let it go. I know you don't like to lie, and you did today, a lie of omission, but you have your reasons. You don't need to be in the middle of anything and Walsh shouldn't have put you there."

"Right, right. And he doesn't know that I read Delilah's diaries," she says and keeps nodding to herself, even after she's done thinking out loud.

"I know what'll help you," I say as I get on my knees on the sofa and face her, towering over her.

She's huddled beneath me, holding on to her beer with both hands and looking up at me wide eyed although there's a smile on her face. "What are you doing?" she asks playfully.

"Hands up," I demand and she obeys, not letting go of her beer bottle. Her bra's a simple white number; it makes her look innocent and sweet. Like an angel laid out before me. An angel to play with, to dirty and taint with all the sinful lust I have for her.

"You make me want to do bad things to you," I murmur. Peeking up through her thick lashes, her doe eyes go wide with lust, proving her to be the vixen she is. Even her cheeks heat nearly instantly.

"You like it, don't you?" I ask her and she doesn't even give me a chance to add, *how much you get to me.*

She answers, "I love it" before I can finish. "I love everything you do to me." With her hands behind her, her shoulders back and her head tilted up to look at me, she's vulnerable and waiting.

I want her to remember this night. I want every moment to be different, every touch to be more than what she can imagine on her own.

I glance to my left and the brown glass of the empty beer bottle glints. Turning back to her, I tell her, "I'm going to play with you, and take my time with you."

She doesn't protest, although I can hear my name and the way she says it likes it's a warning lingering on the tip of her tongue. She swallows it and any argument she has that she's tired. I know she is. She'll do what I want though, because she knows I'll make it good for her.

"Strip down." I give her the command and she obeys. She doesn't try to make a show of it although she teases me by biting down on her lower lip when she drops her bra to the floor.

I wasn't going to touch her, but the pale pink of her nipples begs me to caress them. Her head tips back, her hair cascading behind her. Correcting myself, and ignoring the desire that has all the blood in my body stiffening my cock, I pull away from her.

Without her clothes, goosebumps play along her body

and after she lies down like I tell her to, I blow. That's all I do, teasing her, going from a warm breath along her neck that makes her shiver, to a steady stream down her belly and lower, to her sex.

She tries to reach for me, to grab my arm or my shoulder, but I catch her wrist. "No touching." My command sobers her, and I know in an instant she doesn't like it.

"No. Touching," I repeat firmly, licking my lower lip and loving how her gaze darts to the movement.

Nodding, but still holding doubt in her expression, she lowers her hands to the cushion, gripping it and closing her eyes with a soft moan as I blow against her clit again.

"You're going to make me cum from just breathing on me?" she questions, her eyes alight with mischief and the sexy grin proves she's thinking she'll need more than that.

"No," I answer her, reaching behind me for the beer bottle. I lick the top of it where the cap was twisted on and test out its ridges.

The sound of her nails scratching against the fabric, combined with her chest rising and falling quickly, let me know exactly how she's feeling. "You scared, Babygirl?"

"Will it feel good?"

"Does it ever not?" I question her and the doubt and fear vanish from her eyes. Her thighs part, her heels digging into the cushion as she bends her knees and bares herself to me.

Arousal makes her pussy glisten, and when I press the

cold glass to her clit, I watch her cunt clench around nothing. Letting out a short chuckle, I position myself between her legs, careful not to touch her. My greedy girl lifts her heel, and I know she's going to move her leg around me, pulling me in and showing me just how much she loves it.

"No touching," I remind her, staring up her gorgeous body. She looks down at me, puzzled until I add, "Keep your legs still."

She only nods, her skin flushed and her breathing still not even. Just the idea of using a bottle to play with her has her so worked up. I drag the glass down her clit and through her lips, watching how her hips subtly rise and listening to the pleasure that lingers in her soft moan. It's barely audible, nearly a murmur of satisfaction.

The sweet smell of her, the sound of her moans, the heat of her flesh... fuck, it's torture not to touch her, not to lean forward and suck on her clit until she comes apart for me. I focus on getting the one thing I want... her desire to become so much that she disobeys.

I want her so wrapped up in pleasure from this touch that she forgets the rules. I'll let her cum and then I'll flip her ass over and ravage her. Letting my head fall, I close my eyes, groaning from the thought and feeling my hard cock twitch with need.

Soon.

The sooner the better. Laura's eyes are closed and she

swallows thickly, waiting for me to touch her again. Instead I blow against her sex, noting how her stomach clenches and her body sways from the sensitivity. I want the pressure to build slowly, giving her a higher high than she'll recognize, and then I want to watch her come apart at the seams.

Starting at her clit, I press the bottle against her, slipping lower and parting her lips with the mouth of it. Pressing the bottle inside of her, her breath hitches and her eyes open. She's staring at the ceiling, her mouth in a perfect O when I pull the bottle forward, brushing it against the front wall of her pussy. I don't pull it out; instead I move it back inside of her slowly, all the while pressing against her front wall. The pink in her cheeks darkens and floods into her chest when the neck of the bottle is fully inside of her. Rocking it back and forth, I wait for the moment when her head thrashes and her breathing quickens.

"I can get you off with anything," I tell her and I'm cocky, arrogant... and I feel like a damn king. Her king, her ruler, her *everything*.

I don't stop until she cums. The first time, she doesn't break the rules. She holds on to the cushion like a good submissive when I fuck her to orgasm with the bottle. The second time, she screams out my name, her hands on her face, covering her mouth and she cums hard and fast. I'm relentless though. I never stop fucking her, slow and steady with the neck of the bottle, only picking up my pace when I know she's close to falling again. The third time, her back bows and tears fall from the corners of her eyes as her body rocks and her toes curl. She grabs my arm then, desperate to hold on to anything while she's falling.

Thank fuck she grabs me. Thank God she breaks the rules right then and there.

I barely have any control left and I need to touch her. I need to be inside of her, falling with her.

Chapter 14

Laura

Three days in a row with twelve-hour shifts isn't that difficult. It's not my first time and it sure as hell won't be my last. So that doesn't explain why I feel so utterly and completely drained. Bethany called out, something about her sister. I asked if everything was all right but she couldn't say.

The shift is harder today since I'm picking up some of her workload. The temporary hire to cover Bethany being out for so long, is a bitch who doesn't know how to do a damn thing. So I'm basically pulling the weight of two people today. Why? Because I care about Bethany's patients, unlike Cindy Lou Who-gives-a-fuck and who even knows where she is right now.

Looking to my left, toward the nurses' station where Cindy better be performing the checklist so we can leave on time, the hall is empty as I quietly shut E.J.'s door.

I rest my head against the wall and just breathe. Breathe in. Breathe out. That's all I have to do.

My grandma used to say, *"You don't have to do a damn thing. Just breathe. And pay taxes. Even if you're dead they'll get those taxes."*

The memory of her in the chair in the corner of the living room, pointing her finger at me while she said it makes me smile and it's the first time I've smiled all shift. Damn does it make me miss her though.

I never realized how alone I truly am until recently. No family at all. I only have one friend here, really. Bethany. I'm chummy with Mel and Aiden, but they don't know me like Bethany does. Now she's busy, off with Jase.

I have Seth now. *Only Seth.*

Fuck, I don't like that. I don't like having to rely on him. Especially since all we're doing is fucking. I'm not blind to the fact that when we do talk to one another, it's like walking on eggshells. I don't like it. I don't know how to change it though.

Maybe with time.

Breathing out, *just breathe*, I stare down at the tray in my hand and the last cup of pills. Three colorful ones for Melody.

Maybe some people are just loners. There's nothing wrong with that.

Besides, I have my patients and there aren't a lot of people who get that.

I shake out my shoulders, feeling stiff from not sleeping well and bending over the tray all day. It was my turn to do the pill sorting, well, Bethany's, but I didn't trust Cindy to take on that task.

Before I can take a step forward, across the hall to Melody, I hear a bang behind me. At least I think I do. The noise wraps itself around my gut, squeezing. Something's wrong.

I drop the tray like a fool, turning as fast as I can to get to E.J.

There's nothing wrong with her, though. Not a damn thing is out of place. I swear I heard a bang, like something heavy had dropped.

E.J.'s in the same position she always is, on her side, her knees bent, her hands under her head. I washed her hair today though, marveling at how soft and silky it was. She struggled to tell me months ago, before it happened—although she didn't say what "it" was—she'd gotten a treatment on her hair.

There's no doubt in my mind she's from money. Big money, given the strings they've pulled.

"Are you all right?" I ask E.J. when her heavy eyes open and she stares back at me. Her slow reactions are partly from the medication to help her sleep without dreams, and partly from her crippling depression.

She nods her head slowly and just like in the shower today, she places her slender fingers at her throat and I know that means she wants to talk.

"They told me not to give you my name. Didn't they?"

Her voice is scratchy and I can tell it hurts her from the way she winces.

She must be out of it. There's no way I'd know what anyone told her. I don't even know who "they" are.

The end of my ponytail brushes against my shoulder as I shrug and say, "I don't know what they told you. I just know it's not in your files."

My answer brings tears to her eyes; tears I think were coming regardless. Her face doesn't crumple or contort though and when the tears fall from her chin, down the pillow, she pulls back and then reaches to her cheek before staring at the moisture on her fingertips. Like she didn't even know she was crying.

"I lost everything... I can't lose my name."

"There's always more, you didn't lose everything." I'm quick to console her and I slowly, cautiously, pull out the corner chair to sit in it.

"Do you know what it's like to lose everyone you love? To watch—" Her head falls back as her silent tears turn to wracking sobs. "I have court on the third. For my own custody. For them to take that too." She moves as quickly as she can to brush away the tears, accepting the tissue I offer her. It's a good sign. It's a good sign that she's talking, that she's aware of her pain.

"None of that is in our files."

"Please," she says. Her voice turns hoarse and she lies

on her back, calming herself down, just breathing. "Call me Ella… please."

"I'll call you Ella. It's nice to meet you, formally." My quietly spoken joke comes with a warm smile and she gives me one in return before turning her back to me.

"Good night, Ella."

"Good night, Laura."

Just breathe. It's all I can think to keep from losing it when I leave her. Her pain is palpable and it wreaks havoc on my heart.

Some patients leave and they never return. Their trip here is only a blip in their life. The one time they hit so low that they needed help. That's all this will be for them. I'm grateful we're able to give them that and that their life goes on.

Then there are other people. Patients who are admitted against their will. Patients who are a harm to themselves. Whether they want to die, or just get off on the pain, sometimes they just want to hurt outside like they do inside.

Those are the patients I worry about when they leave. When the doctor or judge says they can go. Sometimes they come back here, worse off than before. Other times they leave here and within a week, their obituaries are in the paper.

The cup and pills are waiting for me on the floor just outside her door. It doesn't take long to dispose of them and gather the last cup for Melody. It takes me longer to mentally prepare more than anything.

Melody's waiting for me, rocking but not humming, when I enter her room. All of the rooms are standard. A bed, nightstand, and dresser. A TV in the upper right corner and an attached bathroom. White sheets, white furniture and soft gray walls. The only difference is the artwork in each of the rooms. And we provide plenty and offer to change them based on patient preference. It was an idea Bethany had years ago. I backed her and we had to pressure corporate to give us the funds to purchase additional artwork. It took nearly a year, but they agreed. I think it makes all the difference.

Neither Melody nor E.J.—Ella—cared about the artwork when they first arrived. Melody decided to change hers nearly a week ago though and I'm hopeful Ella will also come around, although the third of October is right around the corner. And if she's right about having a court date, she may be long gone sooner than I think.

"You changed your pictures again," I remark when I come in and Melody smiles.

"I asked the new girl to do it while I was in the library. She seemed like she had the time just sitting in the back, watching us."

Is that where she was? Hiding in the library? That little... I stuff my snide remark into the back of my head, jotting it down on the memo pad of complaints to give Aiden before my shift is up.

"I like it," I say, nodding one by one at the row of prints.

"They're all classics," she tells me with plenty of pep in her tone. "*The Starry Night* is Van Gogh and this one," Melody gestures as she rises off the bed, making the metal legs squeak as she does so, "*Blue Nude* is Picasso."

I know she's right, because I picked out the classics when Bethany wanted help choosing what art to order. They're only cheap prints, but they're still beautiful.

"I love them. Wonderful choices," I comment and hold out the little cup for her.

Her smile fades and she gathers the covers before climbing back into bed and finally accepting the cup.

"What do you think of Officer Walsh?" she asks me and then lets out a small chuckle. "The good officer, as I like to call him."

The small hairs on the back of my neck stand on end. "What do I think of him?" I repeat her question, giving myself time to think of how to reply while she accepts the cup of water and downs the medicine.

"If you want to talk to him, you should. If you don't, you shouldn't."

"That's not quite an answer to my question, is it?" she asks as she crumples the little cup.

"The thing is, I have to tell someone. I used to have Father John," she says and her tone turns remorseful and longing. The cold comes back, clinging to my skin. Walsh said she was the last to see him. I just can't imagine this girl killing anyone. Conspiring to do so or otherwise.

"The priest who... passed away." I don't say murder. I don't want her mind to move back to the crime and go quiet. Some piece of me has to know the truth.

Walsh's words echo in my mind but they're quickly silenced by Melody. "I didn't know he'd go."

"I don't understand," I say, pressing her for more as I pull the corner chair closer to her bed.

She readjusts under the sheets, lying down as I take my seat.

"I told him everything. He knew what that man did to me and my thoughts. I told him all about the others too. He knew and he never approached any of them. He never did anything but absolve me of my sins."

"Father John?" I ask to clarify.

"Yes." She turns to look me in the eyes as she adds, "It's a sin to think these things, you know? When you want others to hurt... it's a sin.

"So when I told him... I helped..." she trails off as her throat goes tight and Melody closes her eyes. My pulse races and I can barely hear her over the pounding of my heart. *Is she really confessing?*

"When I told Father John in church that they were going to die, I told him where, I told him how and he asked me when." Melody doesn't cry. She merely stares at the ceiling, as if watching, not remembering, not a part of it. Only watching the scene unfold.

"I told him I wanted to be in the church when it happened and that it was happening now." She turns her head to the side, her wide eyes piercing through me. "I didn't know he'd go. I didn't know once he left, he'd never come back. I stayed there in the confessional waiting for him. I stayed there all night."

A numbing prickle dances over my skin. To be involved in something like that... and she's only twenty. Watching the remorse, the confusion, the guilt, but also the anger play in her eyes is frightening. A part of me is terrified that she did go through with a plan to murder. Even if she wasn't there. Even if they deserved it.

She heaves in a breath and the emotional pull of it all drags her down to the hells of her own mind. Her bottom lip quivers and her voice shakes. "He left me to stop it from happening. He said he had to save them."

"It's okay," I console her, feeling her pain, but also my shock, my own horror.

"Why did he go?" she questions me as if I have answers. "Why would he go to them?" Her voice breaks and the tears fall fast and furiously. Unable to stop. Her elbow props her up as the small girl asks me again, "Why would he leave the church, leave me there, to go to *them*?"

The way she says them resonates with anger, with disgust. It's the hint of a side to the young woman that sends a chill down my spine.

"I can't say," I answer her, keeping my voice even. I'm silent, she's silent. No one speaks as the air is permeated with an influx of anger and betrayal, finally ending with sorrow when Melody's face crumples and she lies back down on her back.

"Do you want to tell Officer Walsh?" I ask her and she shakes her head violently, wiping at the tears.

"He already knows," she confesses. "I didn't have to say it for him to know," she adds in a whisper.

I wait a moment longer and it's then the meds begin to kick in, her eyelids turning heavy. When I stand though, my heart leaps from the quick grab of her hand onto mine.

"He didn't absolve me of my sins." She rushes the words out as if she's being strangled. Pain from her grip rips up my arm and I struggle not to show it, my back teeth clenching.

"Absolve me... please. Please, absolve me of my sins."

Fear strikes me, witnessing the dire need of this girl. Watching her reality slip to the point where she truly believes I could help her.

"What is my penance?" she asks as her wide eyes beseech me.

"I'm not-" I start to get out. I can barely breathe.

"Please," she begs me. "How many Hail Marys? He never did anything ever when I told him what that man had done to me. He always did nothing. He sat there. He never did anything but listen. I didn't know he'd go... I didn't know he'd die! Please! How many?"

"As many as you need," I answer her and she shakes her head, releasing my hand to wipe the new tears from under her eyes.

"I keep saying them, but I don't feel better. Please!" she screams, on the verge of a breakdown, arching her back as she does and I answer, gripping her hand in both of mine.

"Fifteen," I yell and then swallow, quietly repeating myself as Melody lies back down, calming herself until she's eerily still. I have no idea how many is a lot or a little or whether she'll even accept the answer. I'm not Catholic. I've never been to confession, although I have plenty to confess.

"Is that all?" she answers sweetly, in a tone not unlike the one she used when she told me the names of the art on the wall. "Fifteen," she marvels.

Chapter 15

Seth

There are at least two hundred bodies in the bar. It's packed for a Monday night. The Red Room is never quiet though. Never a dull moment. Just like Allure. Long legs barely covered by short skirts, hard bodies clad in tight jeans sway and grind on the dance floor. The bar is dark, but the lights transition with every beat of the vibrant music.

The dark red paisley wallpaper that lines the walls and the black chandeliers hanging from the sixteen-foot-high black ceiling keep the atmosphere sinful and decadent.

Alcohol is a constant and tonight I stand behind the bar, waiting for one person in the hundreds to show. The liquor bottles behind me give plenty of light, even in the half beats of darkness. They're lit. This entire side is always lit which is why I stay behind the bar, always watching the moves made in the crowded place.

"Did he say when?" Jase asks me, fixing his jacket as he walks behind the bar to join me and the three bartenders.

"Around one." Walsh left a message on my voicemail. *One o'clock tonight in The Red Room.* The last time we met, he blackmailed us. Tonight should be a better experience than that.

"Good. An update in a public place. Maybe Walsh has what he wants." Turning to Jase, I watch the background fade and focus on him. Freshly shaven with his tailored suit, he looks more like a CEO than he does the head of a crime organization. It's the air around him though and the way others look at him, with a hint of fear, or perhaps jealousy, that give it away. He stands apart from everyone in here. I've been doing my best for years to blend in, but right now, I wonder if I stand out the way he does. I wonder if the way he's perceived now is the way I was perceived years ago in my own club.

"You think he really found Marcus?" I ask Jase, barely breathing the name aloud. Marcus. His gaze meets mine and we share a look. If that list led him to Marcus, Marcus wanted it to happen. We've been following his men for months and we still haven't identified the man in question.

Movement from the corner of my eye catches my attention. Walsh doesn't blend in like the other men in this club. They all have smirks, smile easily, laughing and enjoying the atmosphere. A few watch the dance floor, taking notes on potential women to pursue. Even the ones who are less than fine, and come for a strong drink after a long day, look like they belong.

Walsh is all business. He's always all business. Even without his uniform, he looks like a cop. As he takes a seat on the leather-enveloped barstool, a man in the corner of the room stills, the pause at odds with the remainder of the club, grinding recklessly and swaying to the music. That man I know well and I'm damn sure he can tell Walsh is a cop just from the straight rod shoved up Walsh's ass that keeps him perfectly upright with that grimace on his face.

Jase catches the eye of the man in the corner and waves him off.

"Drink?" I offer Walsh, watching every detail of his expression. His eyes are narrowed as he does the same to me.

"I thought the list would be something you'd find agreeable," Jase comments after a moment of silence. "You don't think it's helpful?" he asks Walsh.

Something's off and wrong. He has resources and two days later Walsh should know by now that the list consists of six men on a rotating schedule doing Marcus's dirty work. At some point, they'd lead to him.

"You don't know, do you?" Walsh's expression changes as he drops his gaze to the slick bar top of black quartz. "Vodka, no ice." Hard, late nights and no sleep paint the face of the man sitting across from me.

"Straight," I answer, nodding toward Anthony, a bartender to my right who's listening in. Everyone who works in this bar works for Cross.

"You got it." He's a young guy, earning his way and learning how things are done. Not bad looking and knows how to take an order, so Jase stuck him here. I know he's itching for more. He's motivated and wants to move up. This right here, having him close enough to hear is more than a test to see how he does, what he does and what comes out of his mouth after the fact. It's everything for him to be on this side of the bar right now. Given the nerves that are evident as he nearly drops the shot glass, it's showing.

"Don't know what?" Jase asks calmly, although I can see just beneath the surface rage is brewing. I don't like to think that I have a temper. Jase though, he's got a hot one for both Walsh and Marcus.

Maybe when it comes to Laura. I have a bit of a temper if she's involved, I'll admit that, but when it comes to business, I like to think I can set my emotions to the side. I think that's why Jase and I make a good fit. I've enjoyed working under him even. Watching the way he does things and learning new methods. I didn't start at the bar though, I started in the parking lot, with a gun in my hand.

The music pounds, the bass thrumming through my veins and the lights dip low with the sound of a roar of excitement from the dance floor.

Walsh exhales, low and steady, flexing both of his hands on the bar. I'm conscious of where they go and every move he makes. Public place or not, Walsh is a desperate man fueled by revenge. I don't trust either of those aspects.

"You gave me six names," Walsh starts and then a chilled heavy glass of clear liquid is placed in front of him. I nod a thanks to Anthony, and wait as Walsh sips it first. It takes Anthony a moment to get the hint not to stay close, but he gets it as Walsh throws it back.

"I put them through the database and got six addresses," he says flatly, tilting his empty glass on the table. In my periphery, I watch as Jase crosses his arms. The way his jaw is clenched is an indication that he's holding back and he's on edge.

"Another?" I offer, and Walsh shakes his head, meeting my stare. It's then that I realize, all his attention is focused on me. None at all on Jase Cross. He's barely looked at Jase. I don't like the unease that climbs up my spine.

"When I got to the first address, I knew something was wrong. The lights didn't work. Electric had been cut. Next to the body on the floor was a note. Same with the next address and the next. All but the blonde woman on the list. She's missing, but her body wasn't dead at her place."

My blood runs cold. *Dead*. "They're all dead?" Jase questions.

"Every single one of them." Walsh's nostrils flare and the

tension between the three of us is at an all-time high. This is fucked.

"If you think you can fuck with me," Walsh practically spits, the anger but also the frustration showing in his reddened eyes.

"No one's fucking with you," Jase says and slams both of his hands down on the bar, getting the attention of a number of patrons. I don't touch him or hint to anything at all with Jase.

"What did the note say?" I ask Walsh, needing information. Information is everything.

Walsh's hard gaze turns to me and he says, "Funny you should be the one to ask. It said: *Was it Fletcher who did it, or Laura's father?*"

The confusion weaves its way through my expression quickly enough and that's when the coldness hits, followed by the heat of rage. Marcus got to them first. He killed the men, knowing we knew about them.

My jaw twitches and I move for the first time since Walsh has been in here. *Fuck!* Adrenaline courses through me.

"I knew of Fletcher and you. I knew that one." Walsh keeps talking. I can barely keep my focus on the words spewing from his mouth. I can't even fucking breathe.

Fletcher or Laura's father. Marcus's note comes back to me. He's playing with us. One step ahead. He's always one step ahead. Motherfucker!

"I didn't know who Laura's father was referring to. Not

until last night." Walsh continues. "I figured if Fletcher was related to you, so was Laura." Jase says something but I can't hear him over the ringing and slew of curses in my ears.

With my hands in fists, I raise them to the top of my head, closing my eyes and praying for calm. He's bringing Laura into this.

Marcus brought Laura into it, and put her on Walsh's radar.

I finally speak. "Marcus... he knew about the list and got to them first."

"How did he know?" Jase's question is accusatory and I sneer at him, "How the hell should I know?"

"Calm down," Jase urges me, his dark eyes narrowing as he watches me. I want to pace; I want to throw something across this fucking room.

"He dragged Laura into this." I can barely speak her name. I feel like a caged animal, ready to attack anything that comes near me.

"He brought *you* front and center." Jase's response is quick and again I catch a tone that I don't care for.

"What does the note mean?" Walsh asks.

"I don't know," I answer Walsh harshly. With both of my hands on the bar, I inhale once, then look around us. The barstools have cleared, no one daring to come around us. When I look up, no one has the audacity to look at us, but I know they're watching. Some of them are. Others are leaving as quickly as they can.

I turn my gaze back to Walsh, noting how he looks at me like I'm hiding something. "Both of them are dead. Laura's father and Fletcher. They're both dead and buried ten feet under."

"Marcus must have known about the list and he got to them first," Jase presumes and places a hand on my shoulder, urging me to stand back up. With the blood still rushing in my ears and my head spinning, I stand up straighter. "He killed his own men because they weren't good enough to hide from us."

I can't fucking breathe in here. Loosening my tie, I hear Walsh tell Jase everything he did.

"Maybe surveillance on your computer?" Jase suggests after a series of back and forths.

"It doesn't matter. The information is useless."

"We gave you good intel. It's not our problem if you fucked it up."

"It actually is," Walsh replies condescendingly. "We don't have a deal until I say so. And this?" he says as he puts both of his hands up and then slowly shakes his head. "No deal."

"What do you want?" I ask him, glancing at Jase whose face easily tells me what he wants. He wants to take that glass or maybe the bottle, any fucking thing he can get his hands on and smash it into Walsh's skull. I bet that's what's playing through his mind right now. On repeat.

"I want Marcus." Defeat colors Walsh's tone and he drops his head into his hands, putting both his elbows on the bar.

"Get him another drink," I order and Anthony's quick to

reply, "Yes, sir" at the same time Walsh says, "No."

"We have information at least," Jase says beneath his breath and then nods his head at Walsh. "His computer's being watched."

"Potential information," I correct him. "There's no way to know how and when Marcus got that list."

"What's that?" Walsh asks. The second he does, the glass of vodka hits the bar and Walsh shoves it to the side.

I take it. Still feeling the rage of adrenaline coursing through me, I throw back the shot and then tell Anthony, "Another."

I can't get the thoughts of Laura out of my head. Marcus is shoving her right in the middle. He gave her over to Walsh. He's going to know about her connection with Delilah. He will soon if he doesn't already. It's fucked. Everything is fucked.

"We'll look into what we can give you," I answer Walsh and before he can respond, the shot hits the bar and I down it, hissing from the heat that rolls down the back of my throat and spreads through my chest.

"What can you give me?" Walsh's anger gets the best of him. "Don't forget what I have on you," he warns.

"Don't forget we've both gotten away with worse," I grit back. "We're helping you find him, against our better judgment. Be grateful for that."

Jase only observes and then orders two more shots from Anthony. "Unless you want to take us up on that free drink," he offers Walsh.

The officer is silent as Jase takes a shot with me. And then orders two more. My head feels faint with the alcohol hitting me, but my mind still races and whatever I do, I can't tame the anger.

Walsh watches as another shot goes down. It burns and settles deep in the pit of my stomach. It only fuels the need to get to Marcus. To be the one to take him down.

"He shouldn't have brought Laura into this," I tell Jase, feeling the swell of anger rise to my shoulders.

"You know what they call serial killers like him?" Walsh asks and Anthony pushes another pair of shots in front of us. When I look at him, his gaze is fixated on the empty shot glass, turning it on the table.

I've had enough. Enough of everything. Jase is quick to throw his back, slamming the glass down just as Walsh answers his own question. "Angel of Death. They don't stop. I may be your enemy, but he's worse."

Neither Jase or I respond. I watch silently as Walsh's guard drops as his true intentions come closer to the surface.

"It's only a matter of time before you do something he deems punishable by death."

"Is that why you want him so bad? The serial killer who got away back when you were an agent?" I goad him, wondering if he'll even mention Delilah.

Jase takes the last shot on the bar when I don't touch it.

"No," Walsh answers honestly, but he doesn't give away any of the truth. The way his gaze seems to look through me, I think he already knows that I know. He's connected the dots. Which means he knows that Laura knows too. He makes his final plea and says, "Help me. Give me information."

The thoughts of Laura and Delilah remind me of the notebooks. We have them. We have the locations.

I don't trust Walsh though. I don't trust his ass and that realization brings me to the conclusion that maybe he killed them. Maybe he didn't find them dead. But that can't be. It doesn't explain the notes.

My head spins and a low exhale of agitation leaves me.

"We'll see what we can do," Jase answers Walsh even though his eyes are on me. "Now get out of my bar."

My gaze shifts between the back of Walsh's loose shirt as he weaves through the crowd and Anthony, who's standing with his hands clasped in front of him to my right. I know he can feel my eyes on him, but he doesn't look. He doesn't turn to watch. The kid doesn't know what to do, so I ask him, "What do you think?"

He hesitates to answer and when he does, he clears his throat first before saying, "I think the note has to mean something, but he's a fucking psychopath and I don't understand."

A large hand grasping my shoulder pulls my attention away from Anthony. Jase doesn't ask, he commands, "Have another drink with me."

"I have to go to Laura. She just got done with work." Fuck, I need to tell her Walsh knows. *There's so much I need to tell her.*

Jase walks around to the other side of the bar, pulling out stools for both of us. "It's one forty. She's already at your place by now."

"He brought her into this. Marcus doesn't play by any rules. He hits where it hurts."

"We may be a step ahead of him though. Now that we know he's watching Walsh's computer."

I nod in agreement, or at least my head does without my conscious consent. Marcus just graduated to the top of my hit list.

"Grab her a bottle of red wine like you said you would and have another drink before you lose your shit."

It hits me that Jase is saying the same words to me that I've said to him a dozen times before.

"When did that happen?" I ask him with a smile, a sad and fucked up one, playing on my lips.

"What?" Jase asks me, not waiting on Anthony now that he's busy with the patrons who have taken up the momentarily empty seats. He reaches around the other side, grabbing a half-empty bottle, choosing to stick to vodka, and two glasses.

"When did I become the angry one needing to be calmed down?" I joke with him.

"Ever since I've known you, you've been angry." He places the shot down in front of me before adding, "You just didn't show it." His response is dead serious.

I pour the shot into my mouth, noting how he squeezes my shoulders and then swallow the chilled clear liquid, feeling the burn flow down my throat and then lower through my abdomen.

Jase takes his and then taps the glass on the bar, looking at the stool where Walsh was sitting. "Now you need to tell me..." he says and his tone changes. Not to one of a boss, but to one of a friend who's desperate to help his buddy clean up his mess, "...everything about Fletcher and Laura's father so we can figure out this fucking note."

Chapter 16

Laura

My shift is over but I can't leave this place. I can't walk away knowing Melody's in there and she just confessed to murder. I can't call Walsh. I can't bring myself to do anything but sit in my car. It's on and the heat is blasting since I was freezing when I got in.

Seth hasn't called or texted. I thought he'd be waiting up for me, but when I messaged him, realizing how late I was, he didn't respond.

That alone and lost feeling I felt earlier today returns. When you're with someone, shouldn't you feel it? I remember, years ago, feeling that security and knowing he was there always when I had Seth. This is different.

I don't really have Seth right now though, do I? I have

him in only two ways. He wants my body and my obedience.

I put my phone away. 9-1-1 was waiting for me to press send. All I had to do was push send and ask to speak to Walsh. I assume this late though, he's not working. I was ready to leave a message, but I don't want to do that. I don't owe anyone anything. I'll write Melody's confession down on the charts. I'll let Aiden deal with it. I already called him and left a voicemail. I already filled out all the necessary paperwork per protocol.

It's not relief I feel when I put the car into drive and pull off onto the main road. There's this gnawing hurt that eats away at me. It points out that I'm not enough. I've never been enough.

I'm too weak to handle any of it. I always have been. Does Seth really want me? How could he when he knows more than anyone how little I can handle?

The green light and white streetlights blur as I drive by them.

I turn on the radio and put the volume up then roll down my window and turn off the heat. A shaky breath leaves me and then another.

I miss my grandma. I miss my father too.

Memories of the two of them flicker through my head as I drive, desperately trying to think of anything but my present situation.

I remember one night my dad told me he had to make a stop before going home. I never liked it when he had to make stops at this "friend's" house. He wasn't a bad guy. My father really wasn't a bad guy at all. There wasn't a day that went by where I didn't know he loved me. There wasn't anything he wouldn't do for me. The thing is though... he did bad things and he got himself into bad situations.

I knew that he peddled pills. I wasn't that naïve. So when he stopped in front of an apartment complex I'd never been in, I was already on edge.

He leaned over and told me, "If you hear bullets, drive away as fast as you can." He made me say I would and then he went inside. I still remember his smile and that should have given it away. I was fifteen, I didn't even have a driver's permit, but I got in the driver seat and stared at the front glass door on high alert the second he was out of view.

My father laughed and laughed when he saw me after he'd been inside for only a couple of minutes. After all, he was just joking. He gave me a kiss on the cheek when I settled back into my seat, and the smile he'd left with was wider than before. He would never know how scared I was.

Not at the thought of hearing bullets or having to drive away. But at the thought that I'd have to drive away without him. My father wasn't a bad man at all and I love him still, but damn did he put bad things in my head.

I don't even realize I've driven to Seth's house until I put the car in park. I pull up next to his, noting that the headlights are still on. Did he just get in?

As I'm walking up to his door, the headlights go out. That's the first thing that startles me. It's always an uneasy feeling when lights go out and leave you in the dark.

The second thing that nearly gives me a heart attack is when Seth opens the door without any notice at all. I choke on my scream and my hand holding the keys flies up to my throat. It's such a jarring quick response, I almost jab myself with the key I'm so on edge.

"Fuck," I sputter, my heart pounding in my chest so hard, it makes me question if I remembered to take my medicine this morning. "You scared the shit out of me."

Seth's grip isn't gentle when he pulls me into his house. "Where were you?" he demands in a low, threatening tone. Ripping out of his grasp, I look at him like he's lost his mind.

Fear, not anger is etched into his handsome expression. Everything about him reminds me how damaged he is. Everything but the booze coming off of him.

"Are you drunk?" The accusation in my tone is evident.

He breathes out heavily. Slamming the front door and moving around me to go to the kitchen sink.

I can't believe the sight of him. Never taking my eyes off of him, I toss down my keys and purse. Seth's busy washing his face at the sink as I take a look around the room. He couldn't have been here long, but still, there's a hole punched into the drywall that leads to the hall.

"You hurt your hand?" I bite out, feeling angrier by the

second. *What the hell is wrong with him?*

His shoulders are hunched over the sink still as he braces himself with his forearms after wiping off his face. "I thought someone took you," he admits to me. His breathing still hasn't calmed and guilt quickly replaces the anger.

I never know what to feel when it comes to Seth. Right now though, I feel sorry for him. He's still in his suit pants but his shirt is disheveled and I can see from here the bruise already covering his battered hand.

"I should have texted sooner; I just had a bad night." I apologize with every ounce of sincerity I can muster. I know the wars he fought, both physical and emotional, have left scars on Seth.

"You had a bad night," he huffs out humorlessly and then covers his face with both of his hands, leaning his head back.

It's so fucking insulting. Like I can't have a hard night because I don't do what he does. It's hard not to be angry. It's more difficult than anything not to engage and let him know punching holes into walls and yelling at me because I'm late—even though he was too—isn't acceptable.

"I'm sorry you thought something happened to me," I say, speaking up to make sure he can hear me as I grab my keys. The sound of them jingling finally brings his gaze back to me.

He looks like he's gone through hell and back. I get that. I do, but I didn't sign up for this shit.

"I'm going home and when you're sober—"

"The hell you are." Seth's tone is demanding and desperate all at once. "Get your ass over here."

My feet are cemented where they are, undecided on whether or not I should have a backbone and leave, or whether I should go to him. The fluttering in my chest and the way my throat goes tight when he looks at me like that, desperately from across the room, that's what makes me put my keys back down and make my way to him.

The second I put a foot in the kitchen, he pulls me in tight and hugs me to him. Yes, he smells like booze. He smells like *him* too. This deep masculine, heavy scent that I used to dream of. A scent I swore I could smell on one of my shirts once so I refused to wash it until I could no longer make out his fragrance.

"Please don't treat me like that," I breathe into his shirt, my eyes still open. His are closed though. Both arms wrapped around me, he rocks me right there in front of the sink.

"I'm sorry," he murmurs and then kisses my crown.

It's then that I remember a similar night. A night like this. One where I was ready to leave, but I didn't. Because I love him. I love the way he holds me; I love the way he smells. I love what he does to me and what I can do to him.

But as I stand here, too sober, too exhausted, too wrung the hell out, I remember very clearly something I told myself for years as I cried myself to sleep.

If I'd left that night, Cami would still be here.

That thought is why I push myself away from Seth, not wanting to cry anymore. His rough fingers brush my skin when I back away. The counter hits my lower back and with both of my palms pressed to my eyes I walk out of the kitchen. The silence behind me proves he doesn't follow me.

Fuck, I can't take any more today. *I swear I can't take any more.*

"What's wrong?" he asks me, clearly having no idea.

"I don't know where to start," I say and breathe out heavily. Wanting to sit on the sofa, but also looking toward the door. Therapy taught me a lot when I was in school. It taught me I should be by myself when I feel like this. When it gets to be too much, I don't communicate well. I know I don't. "I had a really bad day and I just... I can't do much of anything right now."

"Can't what?" Seth questions from behind me and I turn around to face him. With his tie loose around his neck, the top two buttons undone and the one closest to the top hanging on by a thread, Seth looks rough. Rough has always looked good on him, but not tonight. Not the way he looks at me with his lips parted, still breathing heavily. He looks wounded beyond repair.

"Are you okay?" I ask him, swallowing the wretched emotions that come with seeing him like this. He nods, not telling me anything and that's okay too. He doesn't have to, not right now. Not ever if he doesn't want to. We do need to talk about him reacting the way he did though. His anger; his fear.

"I think we should sleep," I suggest, not feeling well myself. "If I look the way I feel, you know I need sleep right now," I tell him although I can't look him in the eye.

"Talk to me," he urges.

"What's gotten into you?" I question him, not liking the way he looks at me like he's about to lose me.

"You don't want to know," is all he says, again shaking his head. The hand he bloodied rises to his eyebrow and it's shaking. My strong man is trembling.

"I'm here, I'm here," I reassure him, holding him like he held me. This time I close my eyes and I let him rock me. I whisper against his chest, fighting sleep and refusing to be anything less than a rock for him now. "I do. I want to know."

"I have secrets," he tells me and I don't know if I should laugh, or maybe roll my eyes. It would be insulting if he wasn't wasted right now. I watch his throat tighten, the stubble on it even longer without him having shaved since I last saw him, as he swallows.

"You think I don't know that?" As I speak, my voice is soft and it's meant to be comforting, it's meant to make him feel better. I know he has secrets and he hides things. I accept it.

"You don't know the half of it. You don't know what I did," he says and his voice goes tight and again he covers his face, forcing him to let go of me. He scrubs his eyes like he wants the vision to go away.

"Seth, tell me what's wrong?" The unsettling, gut-wrenching feeling takes over. Something is not just wrong, it's gotten to him more than I've seen anything get to him. He's scared. I feel it rock through my bones, his fear and despair. "Seth, please," I beg him and he only shakes his head, his hands on the top of his head, his eyes closed tight.

"Tell me," I demand and pull at his arms, forcing him to look at me, not knowing what else to do. Not knowing how to help him and not knowing what I'm going to do. I'm so on edge.

"I killed your dad!" Seth screams and the rage and brokenness that was written on his face changes quickly.

What? His words sink in slowly, like a dark red sky late at night before it all turns black. Shock is a reality. It's numbing.

"Laura." He speaks my name and reaches out for me with both hands. I shake my head, not accepting his grasp.

"You're drunk; you didn't kill him. He—he died in a car accident. He was in a car accident." It was an accident, but my chest feels hollow hearing Seth say something like that. There's no skip, no beat of any sort. My heart has fled.

I rip my arm away from him and he stays like he is, hunched down with his arms out to me even though I step away. "You need to stop and go to bed," I warn him, feeling my throat go raw with horrible emotions.

"I did." His wretched words are spoken like they're true,

but they're not.

"It was a car accident," I say as I take another step back until I'm fully in the living area and he's in the kitchen. "You need to stop," I warn him again, raising my arm. Of all the days to bring up my dad, it would have to be this one. When he's been on my mind the entire drive here.

Seth takes a cautious step forward and suddenly I feel like I'm choking. Just from the way he's looking at me, like he's about to break me.

"He was a rat. That's why." My bottom lip wobbles when his eyes turn glossy.

"Stop it," I say and try to cut him off, but he keeps talking. "No he wasn't. You're just tired and not—"

"That's why Vito was going to hurt you. To get to your father." I have to blink away the shining haze of tears in my eyes as I back away. He's lying. My father would never rat. Seth would never kill him. It doesn't make sense.

"Stop it!" I scream. "You don't know anything about my father," I say, barely getting the choked words out, tears flowing easily down my cheeks as I take another step back, hitting the coffee table and nearly falling backward.

Seth explains, his eyes turning red and a tortuous tone in his voice as he says, "My father... he couldn't let yours live. I wanted it to look like an accident. I didn't want to kill him. I didn't want to, but he made me. He said it was the only—"

"Stop it, please," I say as my legs go weak and tremble. My

shoulders hunch in as I round the coffee table, backing away as Seth gets closer to me. I need to get to the door. I have to get the fuck out of here. "Stop it," I beg him.

It's not true. He's just drunk. It can't be true, but the hurt in my chest, oh my God, it can't be true. Denial is the first stage of grief.

"He said I had to do it if I wanted it to be an accident." Seth's eyes reflect mine. Glossy and wishing what he's saying wasn't true.

I don't know how or why, but I slam my fist into his jaw, only once before taking off. It's all a blur. I don't remember thinking of reacting, choosing to leave. My body's hot and numb and disbelief turns me blind to what's happening. I do it, though. I hit him square in his jaw. Leaving Seth behind me, holding his jaw in shock. I run faster than him, I get out of the house and into my car before I see him in the doorway. The burning pain in my knuckles is nothing.

It's nothing compared to the pain ripping through me as I speed away.

Chapter 17

Seth

*F*uck. That wasn't the way it was supposed to happen. My head's spinning. I shouldn't be driving. Jase was right, I should have stayed at the bar or with him or anywhere else. I shouldn't have let him and Anthony drive me home.

I wish they'd been there when I walked in and saw she wasn't there. I stayed outside while they drove off, gathering whatever composure I could. It was a recipe for disaster. Everything about our story is meant for tragedy. It all could have been different, if only.

Fuck! I slam my hand onto the steering wheel, feeling the stinging pain from the already formed bruises. I do it again and again, just to feel it. I deserve it.

Reckless. I was reckless with her. I never should have said a damn thing. Selfish. I did it because I needed to know she'd still love me after. *Selfish*.

The lights turn red. I swear every light has turned red on my way to her house. Praying she's there, praying she'll forgive me, doesn't offer me any hope. *Why would she?* I already knew she wouldn't. She wouldn't love me if she knew. She never really loved me, because she didn't know. It's why I could never make the first move; it's why I could never tell her those words she needed to hear, *I love you*. It was such a lie.

I was never worthy of that love. It wasn't real.

Thunk! I slam my fist against my window, wanting to feel even more pain. The pain is so wretched in my chest that swallowing feels like suffocation.

I wish I could take it back. All of it. I wish I could rewrite our story.

My head falls back against the leather seat as I slow to stop at another red light. My face is hot and my breathing staggered, but my body is wired. My leg doesn't stop the constant tapping.

Thank fuck the streets are barren. There's not a soul out tonight.

Time moves too slowly; all the while anxiousness eats me up inside. My tires squeal when I pull into the parking lot outside Laura's place. Her car's already parked.

My body sags with relief of at least knowing where she is.

She's safe. That's all that matters tonight. She's safe.

If Jase hadn't wanted me to tell him... If I didn't have to tell him, I wouldn't have had to relive it.

With my fist at my jaw, I stare at Laura's window. The lights are on; she's inside. The sad truth is that it was going to happen eventually. I always knew it would. Her leaving me was a blessing. I should have let her go. I shouldn't have brought her into this hell again. *Selfish*.

"I'm sorry," I whisper, feeling the loss all over again and knowing it's my fault. My hands don't stop shaking.

I did it for her though. I remember telling Jase over and over. I did do it for her. She didn't have to know her father was a rat. Vito wanted to hurt him by hurting Laura, and that wasn't something that could happen.

It didn't change the fact her father had ratted. He was a rat and he had to die.

Fuck, my chest sinks, remembering the old man. Everything was a joke to him. It was never serious but the shit he talked about to whoever would listen... it wasn't something we could allow.

My father knew he had to go the second he took charge and everyone agreed. They were going to do it in the warehouse, then dump him in the back alley.

Then what would Laura have had? She would have known. Everyone would have known with his body being left there and she would have been the daughter of a rat.

I wanted to hide it from her. I wanted to protect her.

Everything inside me needed to protect her.

Then you do it. My father's voice echoes in my head as I stare straight ahead at the bright lights in Laura's living room. Her curtains are parted and I can see her silhouette move from one side to the other.

My father put the gun in my hand and I shot her father in the back of the head while he begged for his life. I never wanted to do it. I didn't want to kill him. I just wanted to protect her. I had to do it alone while they watched. Getting his body to the car, driving it to the top of the cliff, disposing of the gun in the cement pit round the back.

They were going to kill him one way or the other, but I did it.

I didn't want her to know. It would have killed her. She was already so alone.

"I'm sorry," I say again in the darkness, all alone where I belong. "I'm so fucking sorry."

My throat's raw, my body humming, my emotions thrashed, which is why I hesitate to believe what I see. Two sets of lights are on.

My body's cold in an instant. *Fuck, no. No.* It can't get worse tonight.

She's visible in her bedroom.

So are three other figures, in her living room.

Chapter 18

Laura

I hear the front door open and I know it's Seth, but I don't say a damn thing. I don't even know if I can speak right now without screaming incoherently through the pain.

My father's been long gone. I have to cover my face with my hands as it crumples and the sadness rips through me... he wasn't a rat. He wasn't.

They didn't have to kill him; he never would have told anyone anything. He wasn't a rat! My knees are still weak and I sniffle, angrily brushing under my eyes. I can hear Seth in the living room, but I don't go to him. I want to, I want to scream at him, hit him. I want him to lie to me and tell me he made it up. I want it to be a cruel joke I can beat the shit out of him for and for him to hold me until this shaking and the sobs disappear.

He said we'd be together to make the hurt stop, but it doesn't. It never stops with us.

A shuddering breath pulls the energy from me and I hear something in the living room. He moved something around.

I want to tell him to get the fuck out. I want to scream at him and shove my fists into his chest. At the same time, I don't want to see him or be around him. I don't want his large hands on me, his warm body pulling me in. *Why?* Because I desperately need someone to hold me right now and I have no one.

It's hard to inhale; harder to calm my wild heart down. It trips like it's falling down an endless staircase and it hurts. God it hurts.

"Get out!" I scream and the sound is ragged. My fingers fly into my hair as I hunch my shoulders down and cover my face with my forearms. I grip on for my sanity.

Just breathe.

I've been doing it all day, thinking it all day, but at some point, breathing doesn't help.

The bang sounds again from behind me. He's still moving shit around in there.

I know that he's drunk, I know he's hurting, but right now, I can't have him here. I can't allow it to happen. I'm crumbling into nothingness and he doesn't get to watch that. He doesn't get to be around me when it happens. I don't care how badly I need him.

"Laura," a voice calls out just as I get to my bedroom door and chills flow down my spine, sinking into my blood as I stop with my hand on the knob.

Thud, thud.

That's not Seth.

"Come out, come out," the voice sounds, "wherever you are," dragging out the words like it's a game. And then I hear another voice. Two men.

My pulse races with a new kind of fear. Whiplash dizzies my mind.

I could hide, but there's nowhere to hide in here other than under the bed defenselessly. I have a window in my bedroom, but the fire escape stairs are in the living room. The ones made of steel that go all the way down and lead outside.

Sometimes you can't just breathe. Sometimes, you just have to face it.

When I push the door open, listening to the eerily soft creak, four men face me.

Three of them have black masks, dark blue jeans and black shirts. All nondescript. None of them recognizable from their voices or what little I can see of their eyes. They stand in a relative half circle, my coffee table pushed back.

Three men who have come to do something awful, although seeing masks covering their faces, calms a side of me. The logical side, the side that thinks, is telling me they hadn't planned on killing me. If they had, they wouldn't have worn masks to hide who they are.

They came for something bad, though. That much is known from the slow clap and chilled laughter from the one on the right, the one by the coffee table. As if the masks and breaking into my apartment wasn't enough to give it away.

I may be terrified, but a part of me is ready. That little piece that screams inside my head that I should have put a bat next to my bedroom door.

"There she is," he calls out, his voice harsh with brittle humor. I don't know how I stand so tall when they're so much bigger than me.

I try not to look at the fourth man. Swallowing harshly, my bottom lip quivering, I search my whirling mind for anything I can do to stall as Seth moves quietly to close the front door. I don't want my focus to go to him; I don't want them to see him sneaking up on them. In his oxfords and disheveled suit, a gun already in his hand and not on the doorknob.

My lips part to say something as the hot tears slip down my face, but I can't even speak. The barrel of a gun stares at me, the man on the left raising it. Fear is a crippling bitch. She can fuck right off, but right now, she's got her grip on my throat.

The barrel of the gun pointed at my face is a dark hole, like one I've imagined falling down so many times.

The bang isn't from it though, and the next bang and hollering isn't either.

"Behind you!" the not-so-funny man yells to man number two. Man number one, the one who dared raise a gun to me, is already lying face-first on the floor with a hole in the back of his head. Blood pools around his face.

Bang! I scream instinctively. Seth shoots but so do the other two. Bullets ricochet and fly, something breaks and I can't track it all at once. I don't know what is happening, just that I need to move.

Even shaking, I can see everything clearly, but only seconds of it. A second of logic and clarity and then a whirl of chaos. Grabbing the clock on the wall, the large sixteen-inch barn clock, I run and scream, slamming it into the back of the man's head who's closest to me. Cursing, he stumbles, but doesn't fall. I raise the clock again to strike him, wanting and needing to do anything at all, but I hear another shot and then another and the frightful burst of the bang forces me to huddle down.

My heart races. My body hot, I blink away the chaos. My breathing screams in my ears and it's all I can hear.

Seth's still standing. I'm standing. My gaze moves to each of the men accordingly. One, two, three. All still, all not moving. I watch them each again, listening to my ragged breathing. *Is it over already? Are we okay?*

We're alive. My chest pounds, my heart pumping hard and fast. I feel faint.

"We're okay," I whisper, rocking as I lean against the

wall. The bullets weren't clean and simple. There's blood everywhere.

Is that blood? There's blood on Seth. His shirt. There's too much blood. Not like the bits that have spattered behind me. Not like what's on me. It's a circle and it's growing.

A mix between a grunt and a groan leaves Seth as he checks his gun and then it clicks loudly as he heads back to the front door, locking it.

"Are you okay?" I ask in what feels like a yell although it sounds like a murmur, hoping he can hear me. Inhaling sharply, my heart beats wildly and my lungs refuse to move right. He's walking, he's okay. He's okay. He has to be okay.

Everything is shaking and my hands don't stop shaking. I clasp them, trying to calm down, but that's when I see the blood on my hands. There's so much blood.

He still hasn't answered me; he's just walking to the windows.

"Seth!" I scream at Seth to look at me, my eyes burning and my throat sore from screaming. He doesn't answer me, but the blood circle is growing. He's shot. My lip quivers. "Seth!"

He ignores me, stepping over a body to get to the window.

"Fuck," Seth hisses as a loud ringing wails. "Why are they here so fast?" he questions out loud, moving to the window and cursing again. It takes me a moment to even understand. Everything is ringing, my blood, my ears. Shock and fear still have their grip on me.

Sirens wail outside. Loud and they're only getting louder.

"Check them," Seth grits out, his jaw clenched as he breathes in deep.

"You need a doctor," I beg him to let me help him, but he grabs my hand as I grab his shirt. "Check them first."

My eyes are wide with disbelief. "For what?" My head is spinning and my thoughts are scattered. I don't understand.

"Make sure they're dead," he yells out and then leans against the wall.

I could argue with him and I almost do. My body leans forward subconsciously, wanting to go to him and give the gunshot the attention it needs.

"It's in and out, Babygirl. It's not a big deal, just annoying the fuck out of me," he talks calmly, although his breathing is still labored. Heavy and deep.

I take a step back to do what he tells me. Check them. Dead bodies. Three dead bodies all in masks.

The sirens get louder and Seth tells me to hurry, dropping to his knees by one man behind the sofa.

"Dead," he calls out loud enough for me to hear him.

I have to crawl on my knees across the thick carpet to go from one dead man to the next corpse. My shaky fingers dig into their necks, waiting for a pulse that doesn't come.

I stare into the eyes of the man closest to me through the ski mask. He's white, his eyes are hazel and they stare at nothing. Pulling his mask back, I note that I don't know him.

He's just a man.

"Who are they?" I question in a hushed breath and Seth only replies asking if they're dead. My body trembles, not knowing what would have happened if Seth wasn't here. *What would they have done to me? What did they want?*

"They're dead. They're all dead," I reassure Seth as he grips his side. I don't know how I'm still standing, or how any of this happened. Three men lie on the floor of my living room, all shot. All dead. Bullet holes litter my walls, the coffee table is broken from one of them trying to use it for defense, I don't know. It all happened so fast.

"Let me look," I demand, not waiting for an answer. I run to him as quickly as I can and pull up his shirt. He doesn't protest, holding up his shirt and seething.

In the front and out the back of him. Two holes and too much blood.

Chapter 19

Laura

The blood is so dark. Dark blood is never good. "Seth," my weak voice utters his name as tears fall down my cheeks. "Put pressure on it at least. Gauze, let me..." My hands shake and I try to remember everything you should do for a gunshot. I don't have anything here to help him. I need supplies. "You need to go to the hospital!"

It's surreal.

Holding his gun, still facing the dead men on the floor.

"We've got to get out of here." Even as he turns away from me, I stare at the blood seeping into his shirt. It grows slowly, pooling out and then sticking to his side.

He doesn't mention the pain as he opens the window in the living room. The way his face scrunches though and the way he's breathing make it more than obvious to me.

"Seth," I whimper and cover my mouth with both hands. Through the gaze of tears, I see the wreckage. The bodies lying dead, men who came to kill me.

Men Seth killed to save me. We shouldn't be running, he should be getting help.

"Out here, Babygirl," he commands as the knock at the door gets louder.

"Laura Roth," a voice calls out. "It's the police! Open up!"

My feet are cemented where I stand.

"Someone called them?" I blurt out as my head spins. They're here too fast. It all happened so fast; why are they here already?

"Laura." The urgency is clear in Seth's voice as he closes the distance between us and grabs my arm. "We have to get out of here."

It all snaps into place when he looks at me like that. The same way he used to look at me back then. Like he was put on this earth to save me. The desperation swirls in his eyes and it breaks me down to the only piece of me I truly know.

The piece that's desperate to save my broken hero. So damaged by a life he chose not to run from.

"You first," I whisper, shaking my head. "And you see someone," I tell him, already deciding it won't be me. It can't be.

It's pitch black outside, and a gust of harsh wind throws the curtains to the side as the policeman roars, "We're coming in!"

"Go, quick," I say as I usher him to the window. My hand brushes against his side, against the blood. Seth doesn't react, but his jaw's clenched tight. "Let me help you," I beg him as he climbs out of the window and onto the metal fire escape stairs that lead down the side of the old brick building.

He's quick to climb out into the dark night.

The police are coming and I'll be damned if I let Seth take the fall. He still has both hands on the windowsill. The gun sitting on the sill cements my decision.

"Come on, Babygirl." His tone is gentle as he waits for me to climb out too and to run. "I've got you."

I can already hear my defense. They broke in here, they threatened me. I did it. I killed them but it was in self-defense. He can get help, he can take care of himself. They can't blame him for this.

If he did it, if he's the one to go down for their murders... There's intent, drug wars, previous offenses.

I love him, but I hate him.

He hurts me, but he saves me.

Maybe I'm confused, maybe it's the endorphins rushing through me, the fear, the unknown. I don't know what it is, but I rip the gun from the sill, whispering for him to go to the hospital and slam the window closed the second his hand raises in confusion and defense. The look of betrayal doesn't register in his eyes until I lock the window.

Bang! Bang! Two kicks sound at the door behind me and

I suck in a harsh breath.

My fingers are clenched around the edge of the curtains, ripping them shut and hiding him from the police as the door slams open.

It's chaotic and my head spins with uncertainty.

"Laura Roth, put the gun down slowly."

It's hard to breathe, let alone register what I've done. My knees give in and I slowly drop to the ground. There was one rap on the window, one harsh pounding of a fist and I know it's Seth's. But only one and then he's gone.

Run, Seth. Please, run for me. Get help. I can't stop picturing the hole in his side. He'll get help faster this way. He'll be okay. I have to believe that he'll be okay.

He'll understand. When it's all over and I'm free. He'll understand.

My body's hot and still trembling as I drop to the floor, following the instructions of Officer Walsh. I recognize his voice. Walsh. Walsh is the one behind me and there are other cops as well, walking around and checking bodies. They call out that they're dead.

"All of them?" Walsh asks and someone answers yes.

I don't even know how many police officers are with him as he grabs one wrist and then the other. I stare blankly ahead at the curtain. At the spot where I last saw Seth's face.

"I know you didn't do this," Walsh whispers as another cop behind me calls out that *he's gone too.*

The police sirens ring out loud behind the windows. I wish it were an ambulance.

"It was self-defense." I clear my throat and tell Walsh as he pulls me up and onto my feet. He huffs out like he doesn't believe me.

"One of them was undercover, Laura. Your excuse isn't going to work."

Undercover... a cop. A chill travels along my skin.

No. Fuck. No.

My heart slams, skittering to a halt and refusing to go on. I can't breathe. "You're lying." My voice raises as I start to say, "You just want me to—" before I cut myself off. He's lying. The cold metal of the cuffs digs into my skin as he turns me around. Walsh's light blue eyes stare into mine with pity.

"I'm taking you in even though I know you didn't do this. You're going to tell me everything though. You have to. Someone has to go down for this."

He's wrong. Walsh has to be wrong.

I didn't just confess to killing an undercover cop.

Chapter 20

Seth

There's at least three of them. A gun to my temple. A hand keeping the gag in my mouth. The cloth is slipping back farther down my throat, strangling me as I breathe harshly through my nose. With only a single streetlight a block away, I can't see shit. I heard the cops practically knock down Laura's door and bucked back, screaming, fighting, but it was useless. I'd already been grabbed.

The rage is brutal, just like the heat that boils inside of me.

They don't say anything. Not a fucking word as I scream out. The heavy arm holding my arms down around my front grabbed me the second my feet hit the steel grid outside Laura's window.

Laura. The thought of her tightens my throat, a raw

scratching feeling at the back of it. Trying to breathe, the gag slips back more.

"She's all right." I hear a voice behind me that makes me pause. Not the man holding me, not the man in front of me with the gun to my head.

It's taken a while, but my eyes adjust slowly. Too slowly. My vision spins for a moment, the dizziness caused from the lack of air.

Breathe. Just breathe.

My fists unclench and I do my best to be smart. To figure out who they are. Dark eyes and white skin peek out from the black mask of the guy to my left. The one with the .22 caliber. He's the only one I can see.

I can't speak behind the gag, but I desperately want to. All I can do is wait. To see what they've come for. My heart races and my body's nearly numb waiting, each muscle coiled and ready to strike.

I can hardly feel the pain of the bullet wound, but the blood is seeping into my clothes. It's wet too fast. Too much blood. I'm bleeding out.

Footsteps come closer behind me. Calmly. Three to four men at least. Masked and prepared to be here. It could be Fletcher's old crew but the chill in my spine, the lifelessness of the eyes I can see...

Marcus.

It was never Fletcher. It was always him.

Goosebumps dance down my flesh as bile rises up. "Laura's fine. I can't say the same for you." The eerily calm voice lacks menace. Lacks any emotion at all.

"We have orders," the man holding me finally speaks and I don't recognize his voice. But it's followed, too quickly, by another sound I recognize. One I've heard countless times.

Click.

Seth and Laura's story isn't over just yet.
Their story continues with
Tempted to Kiss.

About the Author

Thank you so much for reading my romances. I'm just a stay at home Mom and an avid reader turned Author and I couldn't be happier.

I hope you love my books as much as I do!

More by Willow Winters
www.willowwinterswrites.com/books

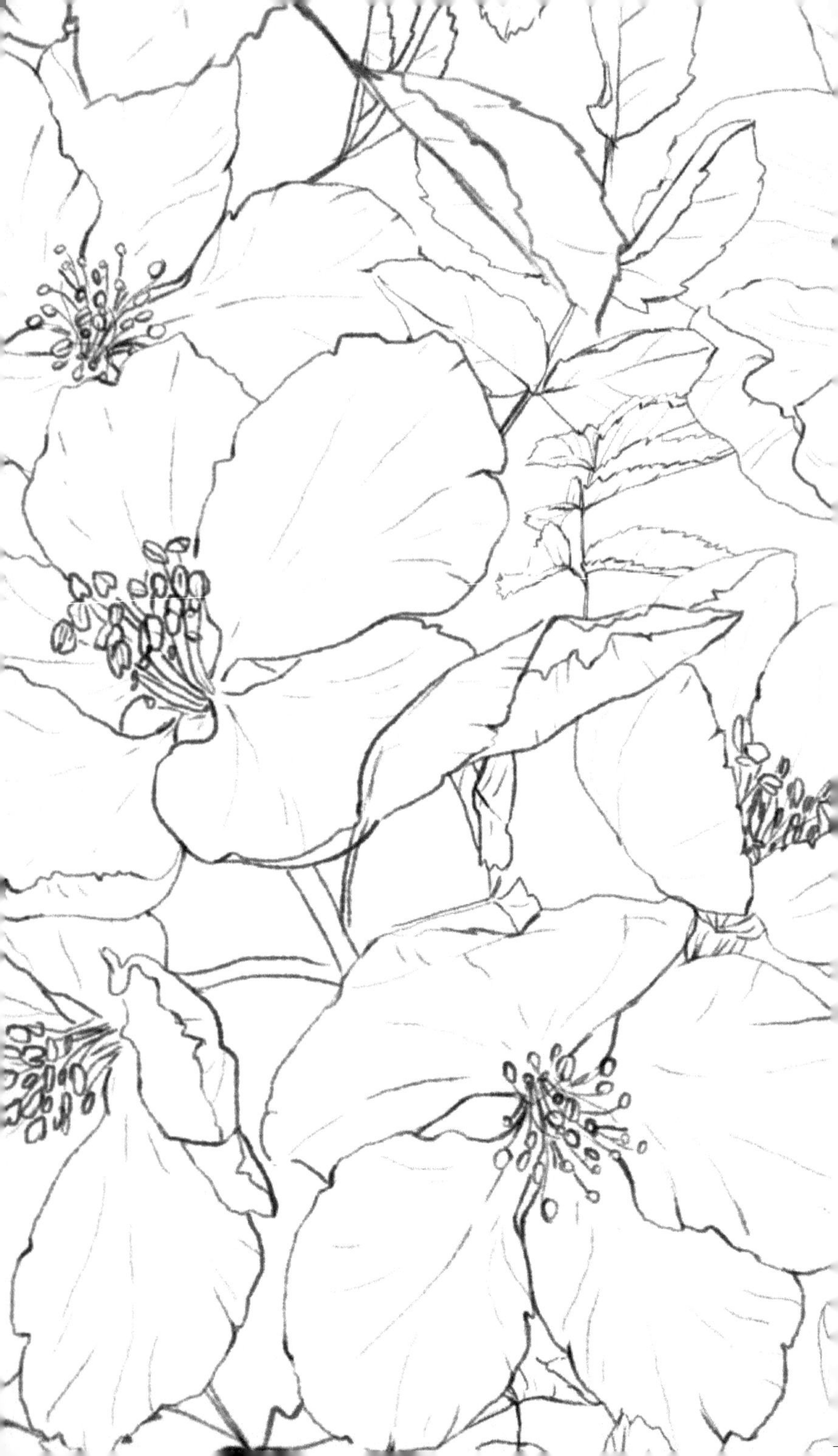